BETWEEN THE SWORD
AND THE WALL

∞

A NOVEL OF WORLD WAR I

Between the Sword and the Wall

A novel of World War I

Thomas De Angelo

Between the Sword and the Wall
A novel of World War I

Inquiries should be addressed to:

Fine Line Publishing
Post Office Box 188
Park Ridge, NJ 07656-0188

Printed in the United States of America
First Printing May 3, 2007

ISBN 978-0-9749906-3-7
10 digit ISBN 0974990639

Library of Congress Control Number 2006911215

to

Michael & Elsbeth

In Spanish there is the saying "between the sword and the wall." Death is certain, there is no escaping it! Yet it is clear that the expression invites us to choose between the wall and the sword.

—JOSE ORTEGA Y GASSET

Chapter One

*T*hree soldiers, gray helmeted and erect in their seats, bicycled into the Boulevard du Regent, stopped a moment, their eyes searching as if they were tourists. Within ten minutes a line of troops marched in their wake. Like waves following each other in a storm the soldiers kept coming. Regiment after regiment marching and advancing. A seemingly inexhaustible barrage of bodies, German bodies, pouring into Brussels. Hour after hour they came, their drab gray uniforms like fog rolling in over a canal. The uniforms, void of color, said it all: the efficient, cold, calculating German infantrymen.

If Belgium were a bottle of water the great fist of Germany plunged into it displacing the liquid from its safe container. What would be left of Belgium, or of the world for that matter, in the days to come?

A drenching rain lashed against the window of the train bound for Holland. Marie Depage sat in her compartment with the morning newspaper on her lap. The news from Liege did not bode well. German artillery battered the port fortress and it appeared that the city would fall within hours. Once that happened the Germans would march into Brussels. They may already be there, Marie considered. She wished she hadn't left Antoine, but the Institute needed money. The patrons in Holland asked that she or Doctor Depage personally come to accept the donation, and Lord knows Antoine had no head for business. Marie recounted the many times she had to say: "Dear, our expenses are too high." It was why she prodded her husband to bring Edith Cavell in as administrator and instructor of nurses. Edith set about at once fulfilling her tasks efficiently.

Marie glanced at her watch: another twenty minutes and the train would be continuing on. The unscheduled stop at the station in Malines, so soon after their leaving Brussels, concerned her. Were the Germans detaining the train? The conductor assured the passengers that it was a technical problem that would be rectified quickly, and then with a serious tone he announced he couldn't, however, assure them of what might happen further down the line. Everyone knew that Liege was the last defense preventing the Germans occupying Belgium.

A small boy in the next compartment began practicing his violin: Mozart. It reminded her of her childhood. An aristocratic upbringing didn't prepare her for her work now, aiding her husband Antoine Depage's Berkendael Institute. It certainly didn't prepare her for what she might face when she returned: German occupation. She wondered what type of Belgium she would be returning to? Would she be prevented from even reaching Holland? Would she be allowed to return? A knock, soft yet rapid, came to her compartment door. She assumed it was the porter signaling the train's departure.

"Yes."

The door slid open and closed quickly. A woman entered.

"Madame Depage."

"Madame Rappard?"

"Yes," the woman answered, taking off her kerchief and revealing a face that seemed to have aged so much since the last time they met. At first Marie wasn't sure if it was Madame Rappard. The rounded cheeks, once red and robust, now were colorless, almost gray. At sixty one years of age Madame Rappard, three years younger than Marie Depage, now appeared to be ten years older. What worried Marie most were Madame Rappard's eyes. They were vacant and scared, like those of a person awoken from a nightmare before they realize it was all a dream.

"Are you travelling to Holland?"

2

"No. I came to ask a favor. Francois told me you are on your way to Amsterdam. He drove me here to intercept the train. I wanted to visit you and Doctor Depage at Berkendael, but the Germans have entered the city."

Marie restrained a gasp. "Is Antoine all right?"

"So far, yes."

"And Francois is with you?"

"Your husband sent him for medical supplies. He spent the night at my home. He is going to be a fine man when he grows." Madame Rappard seemed on the verge of tears.

A shrill whistle sounded and the train rocked.

"The train will be leaving. Tell me quickly why you came."

"My boy was taken prisoner at Liege. He managed to escape and is hiding in the woods. The Germans will find him. You are the only one I know who can help."

Marie's mind worked quickly. "I may not even be allowed back into Belgium. Oh, God I hope Antoine is safe." Marie composed herself. "Take your boy to Berkendael. See Miss Cavell. She is a resourceful woman. She will know what to do. Doctor Depage is to know nothing of this. His work is too important and his health… I fear this will be too much of a strain. Hurry! And tell Francois to drive safely."

Belgium sat like a covered pot on a stove. The lid of Germany's making closing out the world. Red flashes of shells exploded, popping like flashbulbs in the hot August night of 1914 and lighting up the darkness. Edith Cavell stood at her window as frail and fragile as the lace curtains now illuminated by the bombardment. They cast a checkerboard shadow over her face. Lace, the delicate material that is Belgium, could never keep out the jackboots of the Germans.

The air in her room hung still and heavy like it did on so many hot August days before, but now the heat felt even more oppressive and stifling. She took a deep breath, but it lacked freshness, feeling as if she were breathing in the stale air from a closet. Edith could still hear the

German infantry singing *Fatherland, My Fatherland*, while they marched into Brussels. They were moving mechanically, like a large machine with a single motor, unthinking and unfeeling: the product of years of training and conditioning of their minds to be less human. Edith thought of the rigidity in her own life as a girl in Swardeston. England seemed so far away now. Surely the virtues of sacrifice, austerity, and prayer that she was instilled with held their place, but the demands of her father, the Vicar of Swardeston, bore a price. It left her a rigid, serious, and lonely woman of forty-nine. She wondered what life would have been like if she made time for laughter and enjoyment, and of course for love. The opportunity for pleasure seemed now to be shut out forever by the slamming doors of German occupation. Edith buttoned her collar and twisted quickly from the window as if by turning her back on them she could halt the advancing troops and make them go away; out of sight and out of mind as her father used to say. She caught her reflection in the mirror and ran her hand along her brownish hair that now showed the traces of gray. Her thin lips seemed to disappear as she tightened them in determination. It was discipline and the obligation of duty to others which her father instilled in her that would see her through, she vowed. She stared into the reflections of her own eyes and saw her father's staring back.

Before she reached the door she paused at her writing desk and mechanically reached for her pen and notebook. There could be no way of making sense of what the world would be experiencing, but she found a need to document her thoughts like a doctor noting the symptoms of a disease for which there is no treatment. The notation is all that could be done if only for the purpose of aiding someone at some other time to find a cure. She wrote:

> *It is 6:00 A.M. on August 23, 1914 and I fear what is now happening in Mons. The German bombardment of Liege began on the 11th and the city fell on the 15th after enduring cannon fire that began at five o'clock in the morning and continued for nine long hours. The German attacks have been relentless and now they have entered Brussels. We*

*receive no news here and it is only from my treating of the wounded
that I gleaned the true aspects of what will soon become our reality.
Why must this be?*

She put down her pen and remained stooped over her notebook
as if studying a textbook; trying to comprehend. A knock at her door
brought her erect.

"Nurse Cavell," a hesitant voice whispered. "It is Madame Rappard."

"Jolene?" Edith said, opening the door. By the look on the woman's
face Edith sensed something to be wrong. She looked so haggard and
worried.

"Madame Depage told me to come to you. My boy Gerard escaped. The
Germans held him in Liege and when the city fell and those who survived
were being transported to work camps he managed to get away."

Madame Rappard stood aside and her oldest son Gerard stepped
from the shadows. A gaunt boy of seventeen stood before Edith with
the hollow eyes of an old man. Edith looked frantically up and down the
hall, grabbed the boy's arm and pulled him inside. His mother followed.
Edith quietly bolted shut the door.

"You've helped us before. Now I come to implore you to help again,"
the boy begged in a whisper.

"I've helped your family as a nurse the way I am trained to do. Caring for your grandmother before she died is not the same as aiding a
soldier to—"

Gerard interrupted giving her no chance to continue. "The Germans
are in Brussels. I must escape into Holland."

Edith raised her hand to quiet his words. She grabbed her cape from
a hook on the door. "Put this around your shoulders and go to the basement and wait for me. Try not to look at or speak to anyone."

Edith sat in a chair next to the fireplace to begin her waiting. A
small fire hissed while the water in the teapot slowly came to a boil.
To conserve wood she extinguished the flame so that now it was only

the remnants of embers that added a feeble heat to the room. The days were hot, but the nights grew cool. With her frail body she especially felt the cold. She picked up her prayer book and found a suitable page: The Third Collect, for aid against all perils:

Lighten our darkness, we beseech thee, O Lord; and by thy great mercy defend us from all perils and dangers of this night; for the love of they only Son, our Savior, Jesus Christ. Amen.

Her hands felt weary from the fear and apprehension of what she knew she must do to save the Rappard boy and she placed the book on a table. While watching the precision and strength of the German army as it entered Brussels she remembered thinking that not even God could help. Now she cried, ashamed at the crack in her wall of faith. She picked up the prayer book and held it to her heart. She must wait until everyone at Berkendael fell asleep before she could see about Gerard. She rested her head against the back of the chair and stared with watery eyes into the smoldering embers. The clock struck midnight. She rose resolute and quickly left her room entering into the darkened halls of the Institute. She no longer felt fear about the prospects of being shot if she were caught doing what she knew she must do. My only duty is to serve my fellow man, she thought, echoing the words her father instilled in her so many years before. She reached the kitchen and lit a candle taking one of the china plates that once belonged to Doctor Depage's mother. The set of fine white porcelain with tiny red roses around the border was used only for special occasions and there would be none of those for awhile. The plate wouldn't be missed. In the dim light she filled the dish with bread, butter, and sausage. It was almost forty years ago, she remembered, when the Vicar allowed her to join in the family's custom of bringing a portion of their dinner meal to one or another of the poorer families of Swardeston. Vicar Cavell looked at the village as part of his family, his responsibility. Again the deeply instilled traits of sacrifice, prayer, and obligation that the vicar taught her overshadowed her fears. Still her hands trembled and the sausage almost rolled off of the china. It was one thing to bring food plates to poor families of one's village, but quite another to harbor an escaped soldier in times of war. The Germans would shoot resisters on the spot. Still, even with the echoes of the German jackboots still in her ears she knew she had no choice except to help the Rappard boy. A gruff voice broke the melancholy silence in the kitchen.

"Matron Cavell!"

For a moment Edith thought she could see a German soldier before her, but her imagination gave way to reality and she recognized the figure of Doctor Depage standing in the doorway.

"Couldn't you sleep?" Depage growled, in his customary way. "This business with the Germans I suspect?"

"Yes," Edith managed to say as she covered the plate of food. She knew that no one but her could be involved in what she was doing. No one but her should be responsible if the Germans discovered her.

"I expect we will be visited by the Germans soon," Depage said, lighting a cigar. "It seems so long ago, yet it has only been seven years since I hired you to begin training nurses here. If anything happens I want you to know I appreciate your work."

"So much has changed in so short a time," Edith added.

"From having twenty-three student nurses in 1909 to training nurses for three hospitals, twenty-four schools, and thirteen kindergartens you have much to be proud of, Matron Cavell."

"I don't feel as if my work is over."

"The Germans will not let this facility sit idle while there are German wounded to treat. You know there is still time for you to leave, Edith."

"You did not bring me here to quit. I still have work to do."

"Not the work for which you were brought here to do."

"The same work. To treat people, to train nurses. Our work will continue."

Depage puffed on his cigar. "Goodnight, Miss Cavell." Depage didn't wait for a response and disappeared into the darkness, the smoke from his cigar lingering in the air.

Edith picked up the plate of food she had hidden under a dishtowel.

She quietly made her way to the basement. "The Rappard boy must be hungry," she whispered to herself, "and what will I do with him now?"

Doctor Depage took his evening pipe out on the terrace off of his office. He spent regular blocks of time in the fourth floor office content to leave administrative duties to Miss Cavell. When he needed to think he came to the terrace. The view of Brussels helped him to put things into perspective. Here he could suspend the gruff, hardened exterior he presented to those who worked alongside him at the Institute. Most at Berkendael only knew him to smoke cigars. It was the image he wanted. He filled a pipe slowly, each puff being an effort. Anxiety over the German occupation left every muscle tight. He rubbed his large hands across his kneecaps and tilted back in his chair. Moonlight illuminated the spots of blood and iodine that dotted his white lab coat. He watched the smoke drift from the bowl of the pipe into the night air and wondered if he would be allowed to continue his work under German occupation.

The sweet smell of pipe tobacco hung in the air and then rose into the star filled Belgian sky. The whole of Belgium must have been looking up into the heavens tonight—imploring—for some type of divine intervention. No one that evening could have known that their beseeching would not be answered for four long years. Doctor Depage took a few long, deliberate puffs on the pipe. He knew from experience (from the time served as a young soldier in the Franco-Prussian War) that life would be hard on the Belgian people once the Kaiser's men took full control over the country. Being older and wiser in the ways of the world he knew that in every war, in fact especially in war, there would be those who could be bought. The underlying well of human greed would rise to the surface and bribes and persuasion would be called upon. It would be greed to make some people turn traitor on friends and family, and others to cooperate with the enemy. The interest on Judas' silver was still being earned. All Depage needed to do was to make the connections early on, so his work at Berkendael could continue. He took a last puff on the pipe and looked into the French windows, which led from the terrace into his office. Inside he saw the familiar lanky figure of Francois, tall even at sixteen. The boy caught Depage's eyes at the same moment and the doctor waved him outside. Francois wanted to tell him of the Rappard boy, but remembered Madame Depage's admonition that Madame Rappard had relayed to him: 'No one must know, especially Antoine.'

"It's late, boy."

"Yes. I am on my way to bed."

Depage looked at the youth whom he and Marie considered to be there own. Berkendael was the last stop on a long shuffling of the boy from one orphanage to another. When his appendix burst at twelve and he was brought to the Institute he stayed. They hadn't told him yet that when Marie returned from her trip they intended to adopt him legally.

"I'm glad you're still up, Francois. I wanted to talk with you. I assume you heard that the schools will be closing."

"Yes. We were told this morning."

"Do you understand what is happening?"

"I know that a man was killed in Sarajevo."

"Yes. An Austrian Prince, Franz Ferdinand."

"And now we are at war."

"It means that life will get harder for all of us. I want you to be strong for Madame Depage and I."

"I am afraid."

"We all are. Come, it is late. We will talk in the morning."

Chapter Two

The nurses sat assembled in the lecture hall. A quiet tension pervaded the room. On other mornings at Berkendael before a lecture began, there were stifled yawns, girlish whispers about the aloof, detached, Matron Cavell, or the gruff, no nonsense, but kind Doctor Depage. Today the women sat in groups with their chairs pulled together. The fall of Liege and the entrance of German troops into Brussels dominated their thoughts. Would they be sent back to England? or worse would they be raped, imprisoned, or sent to work camps? Many thought that Matron Cavell would dispense with the morning lecture, but one look at her face, with the same professional expression she wore every morning when she entered the hall made them pull their chairs back into the neat rows and straighten their caps and skirts.

Edith looked across their faces.

"I have been giving these daily lectures since I opened this school at Berkendael on the first of October, 1907. Doctor Depage hired me to do a job then and that job must continue. It is during trying times like the ones we appear to be facing when all we have lived for must come to the forefront. Duty, service to others, ethical conduct, dedication to work; I have stressed that these qualities are required not only to be a nurse, but also required to be a human being, a servant of God. The news from Liege is not good, but we can do nothing about that. All we can do is what our roles as nurses charge us to do. So, today we will talk of treating infections…" Edith spoke calmly, but the sound of a company of cycle troops of the *Landsturm* drowned out her words. The German patrolling of Belgian streets began. Edith continued with her lecture and wondered what would follow and how would she get the Rappard boy safely to Holland.

It wasn't until late in the afternoon that Edith could go to the basement and bring the Rappard boy some food and water. He ate without speaking, but his eyes displayed the fear that overtook him. The full weight of the consequences of being captured preyed on his mind.

"This early in the fighting if I am caught I will be made an example of. There will be no work camp for me this time."

Edith anticipated his worries and tried to forestall them. "I will get you to Holland. I have been working on an escape route."

The boy smiled and in his faded blue uniform he looked the boy again. Like a child he was easily appeased in his fear and the worry seemed to slowly ebb as Edith' words reaffirmed hope. Now he began to look like a boy playing soldier. Edith wondered how many youngsters like him were out there.

Edith ambled along the Rue du Canal Vaarstratt looking for the familiar home she lived and worked in when she first arrived in Brussels, ten years before taking the post at Berkendael. Those were distant times. As governess to the four Chambert children she lived a different life. It was the closest she came to having a family. She thought about the four children she helped raise. Her reserved manner didn't affect her relationship with the children and in fact they seemed to understand her better than any adult. It was with much sadness that she took her leave of the Chambert family in the summer of 1895 when she hurried back to England on the sickness of her father. After the Vicar died she longed to return to this family, but they were living grown-up lives by then. It was the oldest child, Marguerite, now Madame Graux, who recommended her to Depage. Now Edith hoped that Marguerite could use the connections she married into to assist her in getting the Rappard boy to Holland. A maid, young and pretty, opened the door.

"Madame Graux had to leave on business early this morning with her husband, but she left her regrets and this card," the maid handed an envelope to Edith and added, "you may use the sitting room to read it if you like. Madame said to give you anything you wanted."

Edith sat next to the large window that faced the canal. In the words Marguerite wrote Edith found a mixture of affection, longing for the old days, a desire to help fight the Germans, and a fear of what that help might bring to the Graux family. Edith wondered if it was the fear that predominated and caused Madame Graux to leave with her husband. At least she has done what she can, Edith concluded. In the envelope was a list of barge captains who might take the Rappard boy through the canals, trusted merchants to use as safe houses if needed, and men to serve as guides to bring the boy across the frontier into Holland. Edith tucked the note into her prayer book.

She rang for the maid and requested some notepaper to write a letter of thanks to Marguerite. As Edith licked the flap of the envelope and sealed it she wondered if she would ever see any of the Chambert children again.

Chapter Three

*E*dith awoke early and out her window she noticed a pall of smoke over the southwestern sky. The gray clouds from spent shells hovered over Belgium like a warning of things to come. "August of 1914," she said aloud, as if planting an indelible mark on her mind of when this all began, as if she could ever forget. This will be a long war, she thought, winding the clock on her nightstand.

One of the younger nurses knocked and brought in the tea tray. Edith nodded and the girl set the tray down.

"The news is not good, Matron Cavell. The Germans are one by one seizing the hospitals. Will we be next?"

"Yes, sister, but there are larger facilities for them to occupy before it is our turn. Not much longer than September, though."

"And us?"

"We will be taken care of. We are necessary to them."

Edith poured her tea and called out as the girl opened the door. "Are you prepared for my lecture this morning?"

"Yes, I am. I find that my studies are what keep me from being too afraid through all this."

"Good," Edith said, waving the girl to wait a moment while she went for the letter she wrote to her mother in England. "See that this letter is placed in the morning post."

"Yes, Matron Cavell."

The latch clicked into place and the door shut. Edith wondered how long she could maintain a normal daily routine for herself and her nurses now that the Germans were making their way to Berkendael.

Madame Depage had been gone six days and returned a different woman. Thinner and more solemn. She arrived back at Berkendael in the middle of the night. After a quickly sought after assurance, in hushed tones, that Doctor Depage knew nothing of the Rappard boy, Marie Depage asked Edith to meet her in the morning.

Madame Depage sat in her favorite chair covered in red velvet with white lace work on the armrests. She waited for the tea to be served and spoke softly.

"I didn't bring back as much money as expected from Holland. Can you make do?"

"Yes, Marie,"

"And the Rappard boy?"

"He is safe. I have made arrangements to get him to Holland. On the first moonless night he will go by barge down the canal."

Marie let out a deep sigh. "I had no choice but to involve you in helping the boy," she explained, leaning over and speaking softly.

"I would expect you to do no less, Marie, especially under the circumstances. Besides, it is why I am on this earth: to help my fellow man," Edith said, hearing the voice of her father in her ears.

"I suppose we must all do what we can."

"We must do God's work no matter what the consequences."

"I am afraid the consequences could be our lives."

"Then so be it," Edith answered, calmly.

Madame Depage leaned her head against the chair back and closed her eyes.

"What else is troubling you, Marie?"

"I have been planning a fund-raising tour that will take me across Europe and into the United States. My papers for travel have been approved. I will be departing in ten days and I shall not return until July of next year. I though of postponing, but we need the money to operate this Institute and continue the work. This war cannot go on for long, perhaps a few months, so I have decided to honor my obligations to our benefactors."

"I will miss you, Marie. Please take care of yourself."

"You too, Edith. And do look after Francois and Antoine for me."

Edith sat wearily in her chair and turned up the lamp, the globe slowly illuminating like a tiny moon on her desk. She reached for her writing paper.

August 25, 1914, Dearest Evaline, it has been so long, far too long, since we have written each other. I still dream of the idyllic months we spent touring Europe. How long has it been? seven, eight, nine years now? You were fortunate to marry and I trust that your husband is well and that the Irish air is agreeing with you. I wish sometimes that love had entered my life, but, alas, it is not meant to be. I have my work.

I write to you now because I fear all lines of communication will soon be severed for us here in Belgium. Pray for me and for what I must do. Perhaps, one day, we can meet again. I close, affectionately, Edith.

She put down her pen wishing there were more to say. With tired care she turned down her bed and flattened her sheets, cold to the touch even on this warm August night. The Rappard boy would not be leaving for another week. Edith prepared for bed although she knew sleep would not come; not until the boy was safely away and across the border into Holland. She unbuttoned her collar and turned down the lamp. The escaping light fell onto the photograph of her mother and father, illuminating their faces for an instant, and then all was dark and still.

Chapter Four

*M*ons exploded as if the earth itself had been turned inside out spewing forth heat and fire. A shell struck a few yards in front of Capt. Boger. A hot gust of wind followed and swept across the ground seizing him like a hand upon his collar and throwing him to the floor where a shower of earth and debris rained down over him. It was what every soldier feared would happen in this God forsaken land. Everyone in the trenches knew that a bullet or a shell could end their time on earth, but they wouldn't know it—it would be over quickly. To be buried in a mound of fallen earth, however, still alive, petrified them the most. Death in war becomes natural and one starts to wish for a particular type of death. It isn't the fear of dying that bothered the men, Boger concluded, it was the agony of a long death. Being buried alive would be a slow torturous end. He covered his eyes and rolled over expecting to lie flat on his stomach, but his turning motion landed him on a grading that sloped into a hole burrowed out by one of the shells. Two eyes stared back at him from the shadows. Another flash of shells illuminated the hole and he saw the face that the eyes belonged to. The man was covered in mud.

"Meachin, is that you?"

"Yes, Captain."

"Are you hit?"

"Just my leg. A bit of shrapnel. I've been here for hours," Sgt. Meachin spoke haltingly, his tone conveying pain. "How is the fighting going, sir?"

"Not good I'm afraid. The French are being slaughtered to the south. The Belgians began their retreat to join up with our forces, but they are hopelessly blocked and so the brunt of it has been left in our hands to stop the German advance."

"But, it seemed to have started well enough, Captain. I heard that B Company of the 4th Middlesex Regiment held the Germans back yesterday."

"Yes, but that was at 6:00 A.M. By nine the German infantry arrived in full force at the north end of town. There were eight Boche battalions and artillery to back them up. They pushed past the positions held by the 4th Middlesex and the 4th Royal Fusiliers. We put up a good fight, but they kept coming."

"That's when I must have been hit, captain. I don't remember any of it."

"Well, by two in the afternoon we began to pull back to the south. The B.E.F. are miles away from Mons by now. The French retreat left our east flank exposed and the Germans are on top of us. Joffre ordered us out, but I—"

"You stayed to look for me, didn't you, sir."

Boger didn't answer.

"Thank you, sir."

Again Boger remained quiet.

"This would have never happened if we had an Englishman as commander-in-chief. Why does the British Expeditionary Force have to take orders from that frog General Joffre."

"Because he is the commander-in-chief here. It doesn't matter now anyway. You and I are stuck here, boy, and it is a bad spot to be in. We have to move. We're cut off. The Germans are advancing quickly and our lines are behind us now. We're in the thick of it, Sergeant. Can you walk?"

Meachin tried to stand, but wobbled. He slumped back down on his knees. "You'll have to leave me behind, sir."

"You're coming with me, Sergeant," Boger ordered, leaning over and pulling Meachin to his feet.

A deafening explosion from the 21-centimeter German cannons drowned out any further discussion. Grenades exploded along the ridge where the British Expeditionary Force had previously held their ground.

"It won't be long before the Germans advance their infantry lines to begin combing the fields for soldiers like you and I, Meachin," Boger said. "I wonder how many like us have been cut off from their regiments."

All at once a quiet fell over the battleground and it appeared that a lull would begin. Boger took Meachin's arm and was about to haul him out of the hole when he stopped abruptly.

"Do you hear that?" Boger asked, not waiting for Meachin to respond. The loud buzzing noise spoke for itself.

Boger threw Meachin to the ground and he fell alongside of the sergeant. Within seconds the ground shook from the explosion. Earth, mud, and stones were catapulted overhead.

"Their sending in the big siege mortar," Boger yelled over the din.

The buzzing of another one ton shell could be heard overhead followed by a tumultuous eruption.

A cloud of fumes from the explosion along with smoke from a fire that ignited in the Belgian woods drifted over the hole choking Boger and Meachin. They quickly pulled up their collars and crawled out of the hole. They began inching their way across the scarred earth, now a heap of rubble and smoke.

"Keep moving!" Boger shouted.

Meachin didn't need the use of his legs for this type of movement and he crawled at the pace set by his captain. Another shell detonated behind them.

"We will be on the main road that leads into Mons as soon as we cross that ridge," Boger said, pointing to a line of trees fifty yards ahead.

"Where do we go from there?" Meachin asked as he continued scrambling over the dirt.

"I know of a church outside of town. We'll see if we can get some help."

Father Louis read from his breviary by the light of a candle. He rubbed his hand over his bald head. The edges of the pages were worn from the numerous times he consulted the book in search of solace. Never would reading the passages that make up the divine office hold so much need for him as they did now. He put the breviary down and picked up the note he had been reading over and over again all morning.

Bishop Namur personally sent the message from Dinant. After Leige fell the Germans entered Aerschot. The Belgian inhabitants that remained in the town were sequestered in the church. A Colonel Meister ordered them shot by firing squad. Father Louis rubbed his weary hand across his brow. Anyone could sense the Bishop's grief simply by reading the man's words describing how houses were looted and buildings burned. Belgian citizens treated like animals.

"Lord, forgive the anger I am feeling," Father Louis whispered, wiping a tear.

He read the section of the letter that told of the deaths of Nelly Pollet, 11 months old and Gilda Genon, 18 months old, who were shot along with their parents. Father Louis baptized them both when he visited Dinant. The paper fell to the floor. Father Louis wiped his eyes on the sleeve of his cassock. He already prayed the rosary three times this morning and beseeched the Lord to spare the citizens of Mons the same fate. When the cannons began their barrage he took shelter in the sacristy to guard the heavenly host and now he sat, clutching his breviary as if the words of comfort could make their way from the pages into his clenched fist. He knelt and prayed.

The stone walls of the sacristy kept the sounds of the war to a muffle and Father Louis paid no attention to the knocking sound until the pounding grew desperate and began to take on a human element. He locked the sacristy, put his ear to the heavy wooden door and opened it slowly. Boger and Meachin rushed inside and slammed the door shut behind them. Boger took the priest's arm and spoke in a whisper.

"We need your help, father."

"Of course, my son, sit down. I have bread and some coffee by the fire."

The two men helped themselves to the offering and slumped into two straight-backed wooden chairs against the wall.

"I think this is the only place we will be safe, father," Boger said.

Father Louis tucked the Bishop's message into his sleeve.

"It won't be safe for you here," Father Louis corrected him while fingering the rosary beads that hung around his neck.

"The Germans will be combing the fields searching for soldiers like us who have been cut off. We must take our chances here with you," Meachin explained while Boger took a gulp of coffee.

Father Louis looked to his breviary and then to the window. "There is a woman in Mons, a widow named Libiez. She can help."

"Can she be trusted?"

"Yes. She has a vacant loft over one of the outbuildings at the bottom of her garden. You will be safe there until you can be moved."

"Moved where?"

"To Brussels and then to Holland. Now come, we must move quickly."

Chapter Five

*T*he cottage of Madame Libiez sat off of the high road and in a ravine of wildflowers. The shutters were recently painted a soft yellow. The flower boxes on the windows were in bloom giving the place a storybook look. The symmetry of the cottage was broken, however, by stacks of roofing tiles which lay piled along the edge of the roof. The first thing one notices during war is the absence of men to do the chores. Madame Libiez could paint the shutters, but the roofing tiles were another matter, so those repairs would have to wait until after the war.

The surrounding area of the cottage's location consisted of the houses of mainly agricultural laborers and beyond that Mons loomed. Until the war Mons was a clean city of well-kept houses, shops and contented citizens. That was before August, 1914 and the leveling of German guns upon Belgium; before the net of German occupation closed in around the Belgian borders.

After the initial German attacks peasants began deserting their villages. They left in steady caravans from Egnen, Dinant, Anthee, Miavoye, and other towns, into the frontier. Now the towns of Liege and Mons were taking their share of the German advance and already citizens were packing their belongings rather than live with the seemingly certain German victory.

The warmth of August days progressed into a cool September and October. The heat from German cannons already turned the leaves prematurely brown long before nature could do so. Madame Libiez left her home early after seeing to the Englishmen's needs. A few pieces of fruit and their safety were all she could offer, but as the man called Boger kept telling her that was more than enough. Madame Libiez set out on her way to Wasmes where a half dozen French soldiers were being tended to in the convent.

"*Bon jour*, Madame Libiez. Are you off to market?"

Madame Libiez slowed her pace and acknowledged Gunther Prust, her neighbor, a man she didn't care for. The fact that his mother was German had, in light of the recent weeks, caused a cloud of suspicion to lower onto Gunther. Prust was a stout man, with thin greasy hair that matted on his forehead like a hat. He had an insincere smile and a constant need to know his neighbors' business. In other times he might have been looked at as simply a nosy gossip, but these were not other times.

The early stages of the war progressed into a distinct routine; a way of life and a reality that quickly replaced the old days of life before 1914. Life was now lived in fear and constant watchfulness. An eerie silence fell upon the Belgian roads; it reminded one of the silence of a schoolhouse waiting for a visit from the headmaster, whose presence was always felt even when he was not seen. Fear and the anticipation of fear hung over Belgium.

"No, I am going to Wasmes to see my cousin Sister Helen," Madame Libiez said, being a woman who found it hard to lie. Here she offered a half-truth. She indeed did have a cousin who was a nun, but Sister Helen's convent now shifted its duties from those solely dedicated to God to one focusing towards the work at hand: seeing to the safety of French soldiers cut off from their battalions.

Gunther remained quiet for a moment and then through suspicious eyes looked at his neighbor. "Give my regards to the nuns and anyone else you happen upon." With that he walked away towards the fields.

The nuns at the convent took as good care of the wounded as they could. Madame Libiez did what she could to help with food and clothing. It was her son, a lawyer in Mons and a member of the Belgian escape organization, who told her about the secret work going on. He begged her to mind what she said to others.

With that thought in her mind Madame Libiez looked over her shoulder a few times as she made her way to the home of Herman Capiau. Capiau, a handsome, carefree young engineer before the war, now played a key role in the escape organization of Prince Reginald de Croy. As a member of Belgium's hereditary nobility de Croy and the other aristocrats of Belgium were left with only two choices: to watch their world of class and society crumble around them or to take part in the protection of what little they might be able to preserve of the old ways. De Croy had done well with his group. They sheltered British and French soldiers who were trapped behind the German lines after the Allied defeat at Mons. From her son Madame Libiez knew de Croy was the man to see and she intended to speak to him about the two British men Father Louis asked her to hide. With a loaf of bread and a jar of broth for the ailing Madame Capiau under her arm she made her way through the streets of Wasmes. War can make a person aware of new sentiments revolving around arms fire. Large cannon and artillery meant bombardment by the enemy and it held its own particular fear, but small arms fire somehow was more frightening. It meant a more personal war and indicated a firing squad, an execution, or that some of the cut off allied soldiers had been found. Small arms fire usually involved the innocent. Madame Libiez heard the pistol shots as she turned the corner that led to Capiau's home.

Capiau and Madame Libiez left Wasmes together. As they approached Mons they heard hoof beats. Capiau took the woman's arm and pulled her into the bushes along the road. Through the leaves they could see German officers with their revolvers drawn moving towards the direction of the Libiez cottage.

Madame Libiez whispered out loud, "Prust!"

"Who?"

"Nothing," she said, and then spoke into Capiau's ear. "We'll take the shortcut. It will give us fifteen minutes before they arrive."

The cottage ahead held a certain calm to it in the autumn colors that surrounded it. Capiau touched Madame Libiez's shoulder and pointed to the shrubbery by her gate. "I saw your Englishmen duck for cover. They must have heard the Germans approaching."

Madame Libiez put up a halting hand and walked quickly so as not to frighten the men when they saw a stranger with her. Capiau came out of the bushes after he saw Libiez talking to the Englishmen.

"All wars have their traitors," she said, thinking of Gunther Prust. "The Germans will soon be here, but this man can help," she pointed to the approaching Capiau.

"There is no time to talk now. We will go to Wasmes and the sisters will keep you in the convent until I can take you to Brussels."

Boger nodded and then turned to Madame Libiez and kissed her hand. "Your son informed us that a company of cycle troops of the *Landsturm* entered town this morning. Someone tipped them about us. They've been here already, but we managed to hide while your son directed them to the meadows. He lied to them and claimed he saw two men there in the morning. Thank him for us. I'm afraid the Boches ransacked your house pretty thoroughly."

"Well, you gentlemen might be interested to know that the Germans are on their way back, now let's move!" Capiau almost shouted, pointing to a column of pointed helmets moving across the far side of the fields.

Madame Libiez son came from the barn. "I've made arrangements for them to stay the night at Dervaire's home in the Rue de la Gare. The Germans will not expect them to go into Mons. I have also prepared to have their photographs taken and civilian identity cards made."

Capiau's face tensed as he thought. He turned to Boger and Meachin.

"I will have two of the sisters, Marie and Madeleine, come tomorrow night on the pretext of seeing the pastor. Be ready to leave with them. They'll bring you to their convent at Wasmes and from there I will take you to Brussels."

Chapter Six

*D*octor Depage waited impatiently. Field Marshal von der Goltz sauntered across the office as if he were a prospective buyer of Berkendael Institute. He stopped to admire the carpet, looked for a long moment at a painting (an excellent copy of Vermeer) that hung next to the doctor's bookcase. Goltz whistled softly and muttered something in German when he fingered the books and came across a first edition of Jacobsen's *Niels Lyhne* alongside *Gray's Anatomy*.

"Why exactly are you here today?" Depage finally asked, breaking the tense (for him) silence.

Von der Goltz held a pair of black leather gloves in his right hand and squeezed them while tapping them on his open left palm. "It is my job to organize rationing and to supply my troops as well as the civilian population," the Field Marshal spoke in passable French. He let out a slow breath of derision when he said the words 'civilian population'.

"Why tell me this?"

"As governor-general of Belgium I must see to the needs of my soldiers."

"Yes? And?" Depage's face now held an expression that seemed to convey he realized the futility of game playing and that there was no doubt who was in charge here.

Von der Goltz lapsed into German and then repeated in French, "I will be using your institute, Doctor."

"Using?"

"It will be most effective for us to treat the not so seriously wounded.

I have heard much about the care given here, especially in regards to your Matron Cavell."

A German staff officer came in and said something about casualties on the Western Front. Von der Goltz turned abruptly and stormed to the door. In a loud voice he spoke over his shoulder to Depage before leaving. "I will be assuming control in the morning. Please have your personal effects removed. Now, I will inspect your institute, Doctor. Do you care to join me?"

"I have work to do," Depage answered, coldly.

Goltz didn't wait for his answer. He had already closed the door.

Edith sat at her desk in the small room off of the main ward that served as her office and prepared the next day's lecture to her nurses. The door opened suddenly and a German officer entered. If they have no regard for Belgium why should I expect any courtesy for myself, Edith thought while studying the man's face. He seemed to be in his early forties and wore the uniform of a general.

"I am Field Marshal Freiherr Colmar von der Goltz, governor-general," the man spoke the words with satisfaction. As a member of the victorious army the man spoke with all the arrogance of a career man. Only a man who lived the military life as a calling would feel such genuine satisfaction to be occupying a foreign country. Power can corrupt so quickly, Edith considered waiting for the man to speak his intentions. Von der Goltz looked distractedly across the room.

"I didn't hear your knock," Edith said, sarcastically.

The Field Marshal cast a look of disdain at her that filled the room the way a fisherman's net covers the water. He began to speak in French.

"The Imperial Cabinet has appointed me to the post of governor-general of Belgium. I am reviewing the premises and will be taking over tomorrow morning. You can expect some changes to be made here."

"Changes?" Edith repeated the word without emotion. She expected something would eventually happen. It had been over five weeks since the Germans occupied Brussels and everyone knew it would be only a matter of time before they got around to Berkendael.

Edith ignored the Field Marshal standing in front of her and picked up her pen. She scratched a few lines onto the paper when his voice broke the silence.

"Madam Cavell." The voice was a deep baritone with an authoritative tone. "In regards to the Berkendael Medical Institute, Madam Cavell," Von der Goltz spoke without looking directly at Edith. His eyes scanned the room and its furnishings the same way he did in Doctor Depage's office, as if he were a buyer at an auction. "Under the circumstances a firm hand and a sense of justice must be combined. To the point, I will, by order of the High Command in Berlin, be converting Berkendael into a military hospital. All sixty of your British nurses will be sent back to England. We will leave the three Belgian nurses. German nurses will replace all of the others."

"And me?"

"You will be allowed to continue in your administrative duties, Madam Cavell."

"What about my patients?"

"Are they German soldiers?" he asked sarcastically.

"No."

"Then they will be sent to work camps when they are able to be moved," Von der Goltz said, casting a quick look at her.

Edith thought about the Rappard boy who she helped escape to Holland just in time.

"Now, Madam Cavell, there are six German soldiers who I have brought with me. They need medical attention."

"My nurses are well trained. They will attend to them."

"Your nurses have already been relieved of their duties. I want you to personally supervise my soldiers' treatment. And I will supervise you."

"Sir. I have been matron of this institution since 1907. I am quite capable—"

"I'm sure you are," Von der Goltz interrupted, "then you won't mind my observing."

Chapter Seven

*A*n unnatural darkness covered the countryside. Dark, foreboding clouds laden with unshed rain, thick air, and the forced blackout combined to form an eerie blackness surrounding Boger and Meachin while they followed behind Capiau who led the way. Herman Capiau began the war with a smooth, unworried skin and the free, unencumbered thoughts of a young man. Two or three women in the village found themselves courted by him, surreptitiously, and he would always be the first person to gather a group of friends around a newly made batch of wine. Now, gray hair cropped up prematurely around his temples showing the indication of the strain he lived with daily. Where he once rambled through these country roads carefree and oblivious to his surroundings he now took in the area around him in slow deliberate glances. One could almost see in Capiau's face the sorrow that came from a man born in a country now witness to the destruction of everything that he called home. The war pushed its front lines into his world very quickly since those early days of August and German occupation.

In the distance flashes of gunfire lit the horizon for a few seconds and then the all-encompassing darkness covered the earth again. Boger and Meachin already wore the tired expressions found on men who have been in forced hiding. When all contact with the world is severed one begins to feel removed from it. For the past few weeks Boger and Meachin, dislodged from the world, were no longer soldiers off to fight the good fight they were now the hunted. They relied on the snippets of information, which they received from one or the other of the men and women from de Croy's escape organization who came to bring supplies clandestinely to the home of Monsieur Dervaire. They never saw the same people twice. Boger asked Dervaire just how many made up the organization that Capiau belonged to, but he only got a shrug of the shoulders as an answer. All they knew for certain was that the Germans were killing the straggler soldiers as well as those who aided them. The group members were naturally tight lipped. Still, Boger and Meachin gleaned a bit of information about the risks and the work that these Belgians were undertaking. It was Capiau, when he came to collect them this evening, who told them that the battle at the Marne River had begun.

"The last report we got was that the German 1st, 2nd, and 3rd armies began sweeping towards Paris. The French 5th and 6th as well as the British BEF started to retreat," Boger said.

"Dervaire said that the French government abandoned Paris for Bordeaux. Some 500,000 civilians also left," Meachin added.

"Well, let me bring you up to date" Capiau began. "From what we know now the German armies met the retreating French and British at the River Marne. The French 6th army was able to attack and open a gap in the line. The German armies are split. The BEF and the French 5th are advancing to fill the gap, so it looks as if the Germans will not be seeing Paris as they expected," Capiau smiled. His face lost the smile quickly when he added, "So many dead though. 250,000 French alone. The Germans lost at least as many if not more."

"And the BEF?" Boger asked.

"I'm afraid that 13,000 of your comrades will remain on Belgian soil."

Boger and Meachin quietly packed their kit bags.

The roads were pitch black and both Boger and Meachin felt as if they were blind while they followed close behind Capiau. A slight wind blew a yellow leave against Boger's chest.

"That could just as easily have been a bullet," Boger said, breaking the silence.

They walked in a crouched position and followed the bobbing head of Capiau through the underbrush. With each flash of cannon fire they whispered between themselves speculating on which of their comrades might be falling at that moment.

"Do you think Hargrove will make it?" Meachin asked.

"He's smart. He can take care of himself. I don't know about Willis though. He didn't train long enough."

"What about Carter. He was good with a bayonet."

"I don't know, Sergeant. It's all in God's hands anyway," Boger said.

"We will be in Brussels by early morning," Capiau offered a bit of hope, and then not wishing to mislead them added, "It will still be dark when we arrive there, but we must remain watchful. There will be German patrols in the streets." He handed them each a pile of clothes.

"What is this for, Herman?" Boger asked.

"These are the clothes a laborer would wear. Put them on. If we are stopped we will be able to explain our presence on the streets. You have the identification cards?"

"Yes," Boger and Meachin answered, simultaneously.

"*Bon.* We wait here. A farmer will be along shortly with a wagon to take us the rest of the way," Capiau explained, looking at his watch and raising it to his ear to assure himself that it was still ticking.

Meachin began to light a cigarette and Capiau gently slapped it from his hand, the match landed on Meachin's leg and he jumped. "Hey!"

"We are not safe even in my own village," Capiau said with a bit of sorrow. "Remember the German patrol at Madame Libiez?"

There was no need for a reply. Flare lights arced over the horizon and the low muffled sound of cannon fire came in waves over the motionless fields which lay covered with paralyzed limbs of broken trees. The distance of the battle masked the horror of what was taking place there.

"Those lights could be fireworks over the Thames," Meachin imagined in a fearful moment, trying to erase the reality of the battle now taking place at the bloodied Marne River.

A salvo of shells hissed from the west and within moments the explosions followed. A red burst and a hollow crash caused them to stop as if it were feet away instead of miles.

"What are my men experiencing now as I sit idly in these fields waiting for transport to Brussels and then on to Holland?" Boger asked out loud.

"You'd be there if you could, captain," Meachin countered. "Besides, if they survive they owe it to the training you gave them, sir."

Each of them said a silent prayer for the men they hoped would escape the death that such an explosion certainly brought with it.

"When will this all be over?" Meachin asked of no one in particular, but directed at Captain Boger only because he was there. The question had been asked, spoken and unspoken, by each of them at some point. The question must have been asked by everyone at the Marne tonight, and there too it would be directed to no one in particular because no one held the answer.

The cart of a somber Belgian farmer rolled steadily along the dirt roads leading through the fields and towards Brussels. Dried leaves became gathered in the spokes muting the sound of the wheels until they freed themselves and the clicking noise began again. Every few feet the frame of the cart would lift and fall with a slight thud, but even that was enough to remind Boger and Meachin of the not so far away battle. The sound unnerved them.

Along the way they passed the burned roadside cottages which the Germans had deemed useless to their cause. The invaders took what they needed and dispatched the residents from their homes. The cottages now became merely crumbling walls, roofs, and floors with all human qualities removed.

The farmer who drove the wagon looked back occasionally, but no words were spoken. It was as if by not speaking it made things safer. By not recognizing the destruction it couldn't be imprinted on the mind and woven into the nightmares that were certain to follow. Silence also allowed for a certain disassociation. Perhaps the driver wanted to keep from becoming too involved in the lives he was helping to save. With death always so close it was better not to form bonds of friendship that would make the loss more personal. Even Capiau kept silent.

The driver looked from side to side and then reached under his seat pulling out a burlap bag and handing it to Capiau.

"There is some bread and bacon and some stewed tea, although the tea may be a bit sweet for your English tastes," Capiau remarked, with a needed dose of humor as if he were the host at a luncheon in his home.

Alongside the road the flat fields segued into lines of broken and burned trees scorched by the shelling.

"We are near Brussels," Capiau noted. Capiau's words were interrupted by the not too far off sound of rifle fire.

The farmer who drove the wagon pulled up the reigns instinctively and the horse slowed his gait. A strong wind blew through their hair bringing a mixture of the smells of the countryside and smoke from the distant exploding shells. Capiau listened for more sounds of rifle fire, but none came. Silence followed, erasing all traces of the resonance of bullets, yet it was an uneasy quiet that took over the air. The distant cannon fire heard earlier conveyed less fear to them then the dull cracking of bursts of small arms fire. Cannons and heavy artillery were aimed impersonally at coordinates on maps by an enemy at a distance. Rifle fire came at a point blank range from a man attempting to kill another man who may or may not be within his sights.

"Even if a rifle is fired blindly it gives me the feeling that the bullets are meant for me," Boger announced with his eyes darting from side to side and then in front and behind.

"I know what you mean, Captain. At least with the shells there is a hissing, a warning of what is coming," Meachin added. He shifted nervously in the back of the cart. "It's the unknown that always frightens me."

Capiau kept silent. The farmer snapped his reigns and picked up the pace of his horse.

Chapter Eight

" The only results from the little sleep I managed to get while riding in this cart are stiffened joints and dulled senses," Boger complained to himself when he opened his eyes.

Meachin remained awake, smoking cigarettes, and he appeared to be the better for it.

"Hallo, Captain," Meachin's weariness seemed to make him giddy. He composed himself when Captain Boger showed signs of being fully awake.

"What time is it, sergeant?"

"Damned if I know, sir. There is a bit of light in the eastern sky, so I assume dawn is approaching."

Capiau chimed in, "It will still be dark enough for us to move and it will be safer than when daylight comes. We will be getting out in a few moments and walking the rest of the way. We are at the outskirts of Brussels."

Boger took a deep breath anticipating the chance of perhaps running into a German patrol.

"Do either of you speak any French?"

Meachin spoke up, "*Où sont les jeune fille*?"

Boger shook his head and grinned.

Capiau raised his eyebrows. "I don't think girls will help you now," he smiled. "Just keep your heads low if we are stopped and I will do the talking."

In more peaceful times the sight of three laborers walking stealthily through the streets of Brussels, caps pulled low over their eyes, shoulders hunched, hands deep in pockets, would have aroused interest if not suspicion. Energetic Brussels embraced the joyful. Three such furtive men wouldn't have fit and a policeman, trained to observe, would have sensed their fear and nervousness. Now, however, they were the commonplace since fear took over as the prevalent emotion in Belgium. Fear stemming from Germany's occupation filled everyone's soul, mind, and heart; fear of being sent to the work camps in the Belgian countryside, or worse, the labor camps in the heart of Germany; fear of being arrested as an Allied sympathizer; fear of being shot by a German officer in retribution for an unsolved sniper attack against a German patrol.

Meachin reached to take a cigarette from his cap and Capiau forcefully pushed his arm back into the pocket. "Not now, *mon ami*. A German patrol could be anywhere. They would claim that you were a *Francs-Tireurs* signaling to the resistance and you will be shot in an instant."

"I don't see any patrols," Meachin observed, in a low whisper.

Capiau simply put a finger to his lips and the conversation ended.

The moon was nonexistent and the streets were paved in blackness. The air, thick with fog, added a welcome cover to their movements.

"Can you tell us now where we are heading?" Boger asked.

"To see a nightingale," Capiau whispered.

Boger raised his eyebrows reflexively, seeming to convey that he was sorry he asked the question.

One solitary light glowed on the upper floor of the Berkendael Medical Institute. A German soldier leaned against the front wall facing the street and lit a cigarette, his rifle propped next to him. Capiau put his arm in front of Boger and Meachin to halt their movement. A German patrol emerged from out of the darkness as if a supernatural apparition appearing from nowhere. The officer in the lead halted the group and spoke to the soldier who prior to their arrival leaned against the wall smoking.

"*Achtung!,* Uber," the man yelled and the pitch of his voice filled the air with tension.

The private named Uber snapped to attention and the cigarette fell from his quivering lips.

"*Yawhol,* Major Grasser."

"A sniper, one of the damned *Francs-Tireurs,* has wounded Corporal Knopfe. In retaliation we will shoot five citizens tonight. If anyone passes on the street you are to shoot to kill without warning and then report to me."

Uber stood speechless. Two weeks ago he worked his grandfather's farm in Bavaria and today he was holding a gun with orders to kill.

"Do you understand, Uber?"

"*Yawhol, Yawhol*" Uber shouted in his loudest military voice to disguise his fear.

Capiau watched from the shadows as the patrol marched off in the opposite direction. "I wonder who will be the unlucky five tonight," Capiau said through clenched teeth. He took a deep breath and pointed to the side door facing the alley. The gas lamps had been lit and a small amount of light fell onto the copper doorknob illuminating it like a tiny beacon in the shadows.

"That leads to the ward where they keep the more seriously wounded. There will be a night nurse on duty. She is one of the remaining Belgian nurses so we'll have no problem, but we must be quick," Capiau spoke in a barely audible whisper.

"Where do we go once we get in?" Meachin asked.

"As soon as we enter we make a quick turn to the left. There is a staircase leading to the upper floors. We take it and go in the first door at the landing. It will be unlocked."

Edith started when the three men moved quickly into her office. She realized immediately that they were not German soldiers. Capiau bolted the door behind them.

"Madame Cavell, I must speak quickly. I know how you aided the Rappard boy. We need your help."

Edith motioned for him to approach the desk where she sat and pointed to the chair next to hers. She rose and instinctively drew the drapes.

"I cannot stay long," Capiau said, declining to sit. "These two men are British officers. It is not safe to hide them in the countryside any longer. Your aiding of Rappard indicates your sympathy is with us. Can you help them? They must reach Holland as soon as possible."

"Do you gentlemen need medical attention?"

Capiau nodded pointing to Meachin's leg.

"Sergeant Meachin has been wounded in the thigh. We did what we could, but he will need proper attention."

Boger added, "Sgt. Meachin is a young bull, just give him some bread and water."

Meachin smiled weakly.

"I'm glad your spirits have remained intact," Edith said, pulling the bell chord that hung near the side of her desk. "Is there any news from the front? We are completely cut off here. Even the newspapers are controlled by the High Command in Berlin."

"After the Battle at Mons the allies retreated to the Marne. We were lucky to get away. The Germans outnumbered us. If our army hadn't counterattacked the British would have been overrun," Capiau explained.

Boger added, "The Belgian Army and the French reserves pushed the German 1ˢᵗ Army back and held their advance. Our British Expeditionary Forces made it to the Marne."

"From what we have heard before we came to Brussels the Germans have been stopped at the river," Meachin noted with a soldier's pride.

"Yes, we have heard the guns," Edith acknowledged. "We are already treating the wounded."

"The Germans are shooting any British or French soldiers who have been separated from their units," Capiau stated and then added, "as well as anyone who aids them. I must tell you that."

"It will not dissuade me from helping them," Edith said, in a calm and clear voice.

"I told you we would see a nightingale tonight, didn't I?" Capiau grinned, pulling his cap low. He unbolted the door and was gone.

The door hadn't closed when a nurse entered.

"This is Sister White. She is one of the few who can be trusted," Edith explained to Boger and Meachin.

She turned to Sister White, "These men are fugitive British soldiers. Give them beds in the empty surgical house. The Sergeant needs his leg attended to."

Boger and Meachin stood dirty and tired and, unlike the officers that they were, they seemed as submissive as children looking to be cared for.

"I don't know what to say, Miss Cavell," Captain Boger said.

"You can write me from Holland," Edith said, turning to Sister White.

"Get these men to bed. Leave my door open when you leave, Sister, the German guard will be making his rounds soon."

Edith picked up her bible, marked by the piece of lace her father had given her as a child, and began to read: 'Into the valley of death…the lord is my shepherd…'

Chapter Nine

*T*he grandfather's clock at the foot of the stairs struck midnight. Edith became accustomed to its sound these past weeks. Now the second part of her day began. The days became divided between her work at the institute—under the watchful eyes of the Germans—and her task of caring for the British soldiers, Boger and Meachin. The sound of the clock's chime barely stopped when Sister White gave her customary three soft, rapid knocks on the door. She entered Edith's room holding a candle.

"Everything is quite, Matron Cavell."

"Good," Edith said, lighting the wall lamp. "We must bring them food and I want you to change the bandages on the Sergeant's leg."

Sister White took the basket of fruit and bread that Edith handed her, but she seemed preoccupied, "What are we going to do?"

"You mean about getting them out and into Holland?"

"Yes. We barely were able to get the Rappard boy out."

"Still, we did."

"Yes, but there are two of them now. Railway service has been stopped. There are no automobiles in all of Brussels, perhaps in all of Belgium."

"We will use the canal, the same as before. I have already spoken to the captain and a barge will be made available for us. Fortunately, there are some not afraid to help."

"Who?"

"I think that it is best if you do not know, sister."

"You can not do it all alone, Edith."

"If we are caught, as we may well be, I will take the punishment alone. I want no one else implicated. Besides that you are doing enough already."

Sister White took a deep breath. "Very well, I will take them their food."

Edith went to her closet and took out a basket of figs and a small crock of patè. "Take these too. And tell them that I have received news from Capiau. The German troops have begun to retreat from the Marne to the River Aisne."

"That will cheer them. They need some good news. We all do."

"Tell them also that I am doing all that I can to get them to Holland. I'll be going out in a few minutes to speak with a possible guide to bring them across the frontier after they leave the canal."

"Matron Cavell, it is so late. And the German patrols."

"I must. They cannot make it to Holland without a guide. I have to make sure whoever takes them is reliable. And I must do these things without haste."

"God be with you, Edith," Sister White said, peeking into the hall to make sure it was quiet. She left with the basket of food after turning once to cast a worried look at Edith.

Edith stood for a long moment staring at the door. She moved to the side-wall to draw the curtains. Out her window a full moon illuminated the street as a German patrol, their helmets reflecting the moonlight, moved quickly yet quietly through the darkness. They were bringing in a civilian. A rumor had been circulating all day that a sniper fired on a German staff car and orders were given to find Belgians who would act as representative scapegoats for the action. Edith wondered if she might have known the man they were arresting, pushing him along like children kicking a tin can over the pavement.

Sergeant Uber watched the civilian stumble. A soldier helped him up and then the kicking began again. Uber flicked away his cigarette. He reached into his pocket to retrieve his last cake of chocolate and leaned against the wall. For a moment, in the warmth of the evening stillness, he imagined himself back in Bavaria. He would have finished his chores on the farm and by now would have been in the small kitchen with a cigarette and a schnapps talking of the work to be done the next day, enjoying the soreness of his muscles that meant he put in a good days work. His wife would have been scolding the children to go to sleep, not because she was angry, but because she wanted to spend some time with her husband.

Uber pushed himself from the wall and stood erect when he heard another patrol approach. They passed by in the dim light without looking his way. He felt as if a stranger to it all, with his mind still back in Bavaria. The clap of rifle fire brought him back to where he stood. Another burst of rifle fire came and the echo lingered in the still Belgian night. He knew another civilian had been arrested for the sniper attack—not necessarily the right person, just someone. The firing squad was given no particulars about whom they shot. Uber thought of the unlucky peasant who would die tonight and wondered if that man's wife might be putting their children to bed. These were the times that made him wonder if (when it was finally over) any of them—German, Belgian, French, English—would ever sleep again.

Footsteps came out of the darkness and Uber recognized the soldier.

"Are you ready?"

"Yes, Erich, I just went off duty. I've been waiting for you. They did say they were at Berkendael, didn't they?" Uber questioned

"Yes, let's go."

Sister White burst into Edith's room, pale and breathless.

"Two German soldiers are going into the surgical house."

"Are you sure?"

"I just left the British soldiers their food and was on my way up here when I saw two Germans on the landing. They are going in there!"

Boger and Meachin moved to the far side of the room and huddled in the shadows. One of the soldiers carried a candle and began lighting the lamps with it.

"Are you sure this is the place, Erich?"

"Yes. They are here somewhere."

Boger cocked his revolver.

Sergeant Uber lifted a mattress and looked under a bed. "You look on that side, Erich. I'll take this side here."

The man named Erich moved closer to where Boger and Meachin crouched. They crawled under a bed. If the man lit the wall lamp it would be over. A ray of moonlight came in through the window and fell onto the German's shoes. All Boger and Meachin could see were legs and illuminated boot tips. Meachin took out his gun.

"I found them!" a voice said.

Boger was about to lift up the bed frame and fire when the illuminated boot tips went in the other direction. The two German soldiers were now under the light near the stairs.

"Blöem was right. They're here," Uber said, lifting two small kegs of beer. "If the high command keeps closing the Belgian breweries so they can use the copper brew kettles to make shells we'll be forced to drink tea," Erich said, with a laugh.

"They'll never close them all," Uber said confidently, climbing the stairs.

"That was too close," Boger said, holstering his revolver.

Meachin rubbed the bandage on his leg and let fall from his other hand a bunch of figs that he had been holding when the Germans arrived and which his clenched fist had reduced to pulp. "I hope that Cavell woman knows what she is doing."

Chapter Ten

"*M*atron, I am so very frightened," Sister White confided, with the voice of a child ashamed to admit her fears to an older and stronger sister.

Edith held out a quieting hand while she stood and closed the door gently. "What is troubling you, Sister?"

"I went to the green grocer this morning and I overheard a conversation."

"And what did you hear?"

"The Germans are attempting to retake Ypres."

"Well, it's October 15th and the Allies have had about two weeks to fortify the town since they took control there. It will not be easy for the Germans to take it again."

"Yes, but still it will be a terrible fight. I believe there will be more wounded coming into Brussels and the Germans can't find room for all of them. It's only a matter of time before they start to use the surgical house. Where will we put the British soldiers?"

"I received a message from Capiau last evening delivered by one of the bakers from town."

"And?" Sister White asked, nervously.

"The Germans are going to search the Institute. They may have suspicions about what we are doing here, or this may only be routine, but we can't take the chance that someone hasn't informed on us. The two British soldiers must be moved," Edith spoke, remaining still and quiet.

"You cannot do it, Edith. I must take them," Sister White implored. "It is you they will be watching. You cannot take any more chances."

"I do not want to jeopardize anyone. That was not my intention when I agreed to let the British hide here."

"You must not assume the entire burden yourself, Edith. I will take them," Sister White said, leaving the room and allowing Edith no chance to argue.

Sister White pulled a stool up to the bed where Meachin lay. She leaned close to his face and gently touched his shoulder. "We must speak," she whispered.

Meachin stirred and pulled away.

"For a moment I thought I was back in the trenches and we were being overrun by German infantry," he said, steadying himself and wiping the sweat from his forehead.

Sister White touched his arm. We must leave here. It is no longer safe."

Meachin reached over and shook Boger. "Sir, there is trouble."

Capt. Boger awoke quickly and sat up. He swung his legs off the cot.

Sister White was about to explain when she heard a loud voice speaking in German. "See how many empty beds are in there," a German officer commanded.

"Follow me," Sister White said, moving to the side door.

The voices of soldiers talking quickly in German and the sound of beds being moved and doors being opened faded as Boger and Meachin followed Sister White out of Berkendael and into the cold, rainy Brussels night. The wind blew cold from the west and a shop sign creaked as it swung on its rusted hooks.

Boger coughed and a gust of wind blew his great coat around his ankles.

"Where are you taking us? Holland?"

"No. Not yet. We are going to a safe house until we can get you across the border," Sister White explained, her skirt flapping in the wind. "We are almost there." She stopped speaking as a German patrol crossed in front of the alley.

✳

"Miss Cavell, you must move any wounded Belgian soldiers out of here," the voice commanded in poor French with a German accent. "Room must be made for German soldiers."

Edith continued to tie the bandage around the wounded Belgian infantryman's calf.

"This is a hospital, sir," Edith said, sharply.

"Need I remind you that Belgium is a conquered territory and the Imperial Cabinet will now decide what is done here," the Captain hissed the words and waved his soldiers to continue their search. "German soldiers are to get first treatment."

"What exactly are you looking for, Captain?" Edith asked, moving to the sink to wash her hands.

The man ignored her mask of ignorance. He shouted in German to his aides and went into Edith's office.

✳

"How is your leg, Sergeant Meachin?"

"Better. Miss Cavell and you have done well for me. I don't know how you can work with the Germans breathing down your necks."

"We do what must be done."

"For a moment I thought we were going to be discovered," Captain Boger said, exhaling a deep breath. "We made it out of Berkendael just in time. Hidden right under the Boches' noses, we were."

Boger moved the curtain. A small amount of light entered the attic room of the three-story home on the Avenue Louise. From the vantage point he could see the top chimneys of Berkendael. Still peering out of the window, from the corner of his eye, he noticed Meachin rub his eyelids with his sleeve.

"Not to worry, Frank. Our only concern now is to get out of Brussels and into Holland."

"We have been weeks in Brussels, Captain, and it feels like years."

"Stiff upper lip, Frank. It won't be long."

"The Captain is right. Miss Cavell has almost all the details worked out. It won't be long."

*

"Are the nurses assembled for my lecture?" Edith asked, as if it were a normal day.

"Most of them can't even understand French or English. Why do we bother?"

"They understand enough and I can get by with a little German. We have to remember, Sister White, that we still have patients to treat and these nurses must perform their jobs professionally."

"Did you ever think when Doctor Depage hired you to administer Berkendael that it would come to this?"

"No one could have predicted that the world would come to this, Sister."

Sister White moved away from the door and closer to the writing desk where Edith sat with pen in hand.

Edith's face remained stoic, but her hand trembled a bit.

"You cannot do all this by yourself, Edith. We have three Belgian nurses, surely we can trust them to help."

"I can not do that, Sister. If the Germans find us it will be only me they can arrest."

"In my heart I just know that they know about us," Sister White held back a tear.

"If they were sure they would have arrested me," Edith answered, in a level voice.

Sister White, her legs shaking slightly, steadied herself on the mahogany bedpost and then sat on the edge of the bed.

"That is why I want you to leave here, Sister," Edith said, calmly. "As soon as we can move them from the Avenue Louise and into Holland you shall accompany them."

Sister White gave a start. "Leave?"

"Yes. It is too dangerous for you at the Institute, I can't subject you to the danger."

"For you also, Edith," Sister White's voice cracked with emotion.

Edith put her pen to the sheet of paper in front of her. The room went silent with only the sound of Edith's pen scratching quickly across the page.

> *Mother, I thought and prayed that I would be spending Christmas with you in Norwich. Now I see no hope for that happy reunion. The Germans are in complete control here. Who could have predicted last time we were together that 1914 would be so horrific a time? What will be in 1915, 1916, 1917... You must be asking yourself as we all are when this war will end. Father would have said it is in God's hands as we all are. I cannot send this message by post for fear that the Germans will intercept it. Sister White is carrying this bit of news to you and I trust that you will show her all the kindness and affection you would your own daughter. She is a good woman, but do not let her stories worry you. I will be in your garden in a not too distant spring, weeding and making room for the primrose and geraniums. With love, Edith.*

Edith folded the note carefully and sealed it in an envelope. She placed the envelope in a larger one that already held papers. "You will take this with you, Helen. The envelope is for my mother and the rest are notes that Captain Boger has compiled for the British."

Edith looked out her window and across the Avenue Louise. "We must move them across the border into Holland," she said in a low voice.

Chapter Eleven

*H*erman Capiau sat hunched over and squatting in the heather fields. He had the wick of his lantern lowered to the point where if it went down even one more centimeter the light would have been extinguished. He looked to the west. Whatever was happening tonight in Brussels was in God's hands. Were the English soldiers still undiscovered or did the Germans find them? He whispered a prayer for God's help for the Cavell woman. It was anyone's guess what was happening further on past Brussels and beyond the Flemish lowlands. The flat and fertile land of his boyhood was now being flooded as the sluices were being opened to flood the land and hopefully stop the German advance. Beaches, dunes, conifer woods, ponds, marshes, pastures, corn fields, all of it being drowned to stop what men, and particularly the Belgian and French and English men, could not seem to stop: the advancing jackboots of the German invaders.

Herman closed his eyes and let the scent of the Sambre and the Meuse fill his nose. The waters still ran clean, but for how long? Would they too be bloodied like the Marne? The scent of pine blew in from across the Soignes, the old Forest of Cologne that saw the Romans come in ancient time and now witnessed another breed of men looking to conquer the world. He heard the muffled steps of someone moving slowly and deliberately. He put his wrist close to the flame and read the dial of his watch. The time was right, it had to be de Croy. He listened for the signal of two stones being tossed into the fields. One came and then the other. Capiau stood slowly and called out, "To your left," when he saw the dim light of de Croy's own lantern.

Prince Reginald de Croy, tall and aristocratic, eased through the heather bushes with the same grace as if he were gliding through one of the ballrooms of Brussels in another time when the aristocracy had only to consider its own pleasures. de Croy walked slightly stooped now, yet with a regal bearing that one only attains from years of attending the best schools and partaking in the privileges of a wealthy lifestyle. It was de Croy's leadership that allowed the organization to continue the dangerous task at hand. Also his money and contacts were given freely to aid the resistance.

"Herman," de Croy said, patting the man's knee and joining him in a squatting position in the bushes.

"It was a bad day yesterday, my friend."

"It is fitting that today is All Soul's day. We have lost many at Ypres. It will be a long and costly battle."

"It will be a long and costly war," de Croy spoke to the darkness.

"Perhaps the next few days will find the allies decisive in Ypres and in the rest of the war," Capiau said, staring into the darkened sky.

"The last word was that the Germans are pouring through the Gheluvelt gap and pressing hard on the left flank of the 1st Cavalry Division."

"Has Foch been able to send reinforcements?"

"No, not yet."

Capiau sucked on his pipe and watched the heather sway in the light November breeze. "Why this meeting?"

"We have gathered a group of soldiers that you must place in safe houses," de Croy explained.

"A group?" Capiau repeated, being familiar with finding only one or two soldiers at a time separated from their regiments and lost in the fields.

"Yes, seven English privates," de Croy said, with a concerned look on his tightly drawn face.

"Seven?" Capiau said the word and sat on the ground with a deep expulsion of air. A thought crossed his mind, "I wonder if Sister Cavell can help?"

de Croy ignored the worry in Capiau's voice and stood slightly, waving his lantern as he rose.

A short man came from the shadows.

"This is Phillipe Baucq, an architect from Brussels. He is joining our organization."

Phillipe Baucq extended his hand with a smile. His thick lips parted in a wide grin. He had the clear unwrinkled skin of youth. Baucq disregarded Herman Capiau's look of suspicion. "I have drawn up a map of the latest German patrol movements through Brussels. It should assist you in aiding the escaping allied soldiers," Baucq said, reaching into each of his pockets. "I had it here somewhere."

"A bit disorganized for an architect," Capiau said with a smile, but his voice betrayed his concern.

Baucq shoved his hands into his pockets. Capiau couldn't help but notice that the man's wardrobe looked thrown together by a blind man: the pants were expensive and the coat an old cloth one. The shoes, also of high quality looked to have never been polished. Capiau sensed that the man was of an absentminded disposition. Capiau pulled de Croy's sleeve and whispered, "How can a man so obviously disorganized be of assistance in the dangerous and exacting endeavors that our organization is involved in?"

de Croy waived a dismissive hand. Capiau muttered to himself, "This man will be our downfall."

"Here it is," Baucq said, unraveling the hand drawn map from a crumpled handkerchief.

de Croy took the map. "Thank you, Phillipe, you can leave first. We'll follow along in five minutes and meet you at the truck."

Capiau watched as Baucq disappeared into the shadows. de Croy watched Capiau.

"Don't worry, Herman. He can be trained. He will be invaluable to our goals. And don't forget he too is willing to risk his life for Belgium."

Capiau remained silent raising an eyebrow. "It's been five minutes, shall we follow?" he said, not waiting for an answer from de Croy and slipping into the darkness.

Chapter Twelve

"*I* don't like it, Marie," Doctor Depage said, while wiping his mouth with a napkin and finishing what remained of the dinner wine in his glass.

"Antoine, we have been over this. I've already delayed my trip over a month. It's the second week of December and I've missed important meetings in New York. Berkendael needs the money."

"You talk as if we had a choice. It's not like the Germans are imaginary. They are quite real. They could change their mind or stop you along the way."

Doctor Depage displayed a painful smile while striking a match to light his pipe. "I don't like it."

"Antoine, you are getting yourself excited."

"I had to pay von Bissing himself for the travel papers to be stamped."

"It seems that it was easier dealing with Field Marshall Von der Goltz."

"They are all alike, my dear. We are like Marionettes in the hands of the Germans. Von Bissing has only been in charge about two weeks and I already feel things will be tightening up. Ever since the Germans were stopped at the Marne and then lost Ypres the High Command in Berlin has been getting nervous. That will be passed on to us poor Belgians. In another week you would not be allowed to travel. Once von Bissing settles in permanently things will change."

"Well, you did manage it, Antoine, and that is all that matters. This fund raising tour in America is crucial to Berkendael and your work."

Doctor Depage couldn't dispute his wife's remark.

"Still, I will miss you, Marie."

"And I you, but we both know I must go. You are too needed here to make the trip yourself. That leaves only me to go."

Doctor Depage kissed his wife and sat down next to her.

"How long do you think this war will go on, Antoine? Certainly it will be over by the time I return in the summer."

"It will not be ended by the summer of 1915, Marie, or by the summer of 1916 or 1917 for that matter. I see no end to this madness. Both sides are in the trenches which act like locked doors that neither side can penetrate."

The doctor stood when he heard a knock at the door. Since the Germans arrived even a simple knock was enough to cause panic. He walked apprehensively to the door.

"Madame Depage, Francois has your bags in the car," Sister White said.

"Thank you, Sister, tell him I am on my way down." Madame Depage turned to her husband. "It must have cost dearly for that car, Antoine. Should you have?"

"I could find no other way. There are no taxis or private cars. I had to 'rent' a car from von Bissing," Doctor Depage turned to the window.

"Antoine, is that a tear? You are such a sweet man under all that gruffness you portray to your nurses."

Depage hugged her. "Perhaps I should say goodbye here. I wouldn't want to spoil my image."

"Yes, dear, that would be better. I only have one regret. This Christmas of 1914 will be our first apart."

"Well, we'll make it up next year."

"Yes, we will. Please watch out for Francois while I am gone."

"The orphanage says we can arrange the adoption papers when you return, but I haven't mentioned it to him."

"He'll be so happy. Goodbye, Antoine."

Francois stood, thin and straight, with an ever present smile. He tried to convey strength, but his lips quivered as he hugged Madame Depage.

"I have spoken to Monsieur Depage and he has assured me you will be put to task if you slacken in your studies," Madame Depage feigned seriousness that soon broke into a smile.

"With all the work I do here who has time to study?" Francois said with a grin.

Madame Depage whispered to him. "Take care of each other while I am gone."

"Yes, Madame, we will. I promise."

"Marie, you take care of yourself," Edith said, walking Madame Depage to the car.

Edith watched Madame Depage's car move slowly down the street. She turned reluctantly and walked towards the front doors of the Institute. Before she reached the steps she stopped suddenly as the sounds of rapid rifle fire cracked. From the sharpness of the sound it appeared that the firing was close by.

"Bring him in here," a soldier yelled in German.

A stretcher came into view and Edith motioned for her nurses, who had all congregated outside to watch Madame Depage leave, to go back to their duties.

She, and Francois, stood at the entrance as soldiers came from each direction of the street.

"This man needs attention. He has been wounded."

"Yes, certainly. Bring him in," Edith said.

The stretcher passed in front of Edith and she saw blood on the man's shoulder. He spoke, "It is a minor wound."

"We'll look at it immediately."

The officer in charge looked with hateful eyes at Edith. "It is the damned *Francs-Tireurs* who are responsible for this."

Edith didn't answer.

The officer looked at the wounded man. "Sergeant Uber, you will be treated well. We have German nurses inside."

"I assure you that all of my nurses, Belgian or German are capable."

The officer interrupted. "See that only German nurses tend to Sergeant Uber. I am going to join my patrol and search for the sniper who did this."

The man was about to leave when he turned to Francois. He yanked the boy's collar. If the sniper is not found I am sure there will be witnesses who will identify you as the guilty one."

Francois gave a frightened look at Edith while the officer pulled him towards the waiting German patrol.

Chapter Thirteen

A walk that would usually have taken ten minutes now took an hour. Edith strolled as slowly and quietly as she could with frequent stops in the shadows of doorways or quick retreats into a convenient alley. This last part of the plan, to get Boger and Meachin a guide into Holland, seemed the most nerve racking. Was she being followed? Would she be arrested? Edith moved anxiously through the deserted streets of Brussels. She crouched in a cellar stairway when she heard voices in low muffled German. A group of soldiers were pulling two army wagons that would be needing repair in the morning and they were looking for a suitable place on the side of the road to leave it. Supplies were now constantly being carried through the streets on such wagons bound for the railway stations, and destined for the front lines. While Edith waited for the soldiers to deposit their load and leave she thought, an unsettling and anxious thought about the fate of Francois. He was just a boy, surely the Germans would release him in the morning. Depage would be able to help. He could arrange to have Francois released. A gift of money could be sent to von Bissing. A cold breeze brought a scent of moisture to her nostrils and she wondered if Marie safely boarded her passage to America. One of the German soldiers instigated a fight with another and they were stumbling in her direction. Her heart raced when she saw the moonlight reflected in the buttons of the soldiers' uniforms. They were that close. One of the clearer headed of the group suggested that they settle it over a beer and, begrudgingly, the two opponents shook hands and stumbled away into the darkness.

It took five minutes for Edith to summon the courage to move from her position in the shadows. When she reached the apartment house it was three in the morning. The rear door hung open as arranged and a few small candles lit the way to the fourth floor. The door to apartment 414 was open and Louis Pretre waited at the entrance. He pulled her in and closed the door.

"Did anyone see you?"

"No."

Pretre stood a tall and bulky man dressed in the clothes of a fisherman. His large yellow mustache matched the great mane of yellow hair that sat above his tanned and lined face. It appeared almost comical to see such a large man so afraid. All of Belgium, all of the world, was afraid.

"I have settled on a plan," Louis began, tapping his pipe on his palm. "We will take a sideways route to Louvain and then backtrack to Malines, into Lier, and then Antwerp and the border. I have the schedules of the German patrols and we should miss each one if I timed it right. I also made a list of where troops are encamped. Once the timing is right we'll split up and one will go on by way of the canal on the barge you arranged for. I'll take the other across the frontier. I think the three of us will be fine."

"There will be four," Edith said calmly.

Louis re-lit his pipe. "Have you decided to escape?"

"No, I am sending Sister White. It has become too dangerous for her here."

"Very well, one more won't matter. But only one more."

Edith took out a purse and handed it to Pretre.

"There is enough for your fee as well as for supplies."

"Thank you, but if we are caught no amount of money will save us."

Edith took a deep breath. "I need all of your notes about patrol times and troop encampments. I want Sister White to bring them to England. It could prove useful to the Allies."

"You know you can be shot for this?"

"I would not be of much worth if I stayed alive only because of the fact that I didn't help." For a moment Edith could hear her father's voice, praying.

Sister White awoke in a feverish sweat. Her heart raced and her hands trembled when she attempted to put them together to pray. "Oh, dear God, help me." She lowered her head and felt her shaking fingers on her forehead. She raised her voice leaving no chance that God might mishear her plea.

The halls of Berkendael seemed strange as if they no longer belonged to her life. Sister White moved slowly and quietly to Edith's room remembering as she went. A photograph of Edith and Doctor Depage on the day she arrived in 1907 to take over the training of nurses at Berkendael hung near the stairs. A small stain on the carpet at the foot of the steps recalled the time Francois spilled a vial of Doctor Depage's chemicals. The sound of two of the German nurses speaking in hushed tones near the kitchen made her realize just how far away those days of pre-war Belgium were.

Edith met her at the top of the landing and they slipped silently down the hall. When Edith closed the door Sister White spoke.

"Edith, I wish you would reconsider and come with us."

"The plans have already been made."

Edith sat at her desk and began to sort and collect papers. Sister White moved to the window. What began as a cold, clear December day turned dark by afternoon and then the rains came. Sister White peered out of the drapes towards the Avenue Louise and the building where Boger and Meachin waited. A medieval gargoyle that sat on the edifice of the apartment glistened in the moonlight and dripped water like tears. She was momentarily startled when Edith touched her lightly on the shoulder as if she were being summoned from a dream.

"I have the papers that Louis Pretre gave me. There are also drawings that Captain Boger made of the battlefields. If Boger or Meachin were caught with these they would be shot on the spot. I'm afraid it won't be any better for you, Sister."

With a firm, unhesitating hand Sister White took the papers and stuffed them under her blouse.

They sat in the window seat, not speaking, as the last of the German patrols passed under the window.

"It is time," Edith said, breaking the silence.

"Yes, it is," Sister White agreed after taking a deep breath.

The Avenue Louis was covered with rain water as if it were a small river. Edith insisted on accompanying her to the apartment and then in the darkness retreated to Berkendael. Sister White moved cautiously through the shadows. She could already feel her toes numbing with cold and there was still so far to go. A German soldier stumbled out of a tavern across the road and moved shakily in the other direction. The streets were darkened in observance of the blackout. Ahead she could see a flickering of light coming from an opening and closing shade. Boger and Meachin were ready. From nowhere a large figure emerged from the darkness. Louis Pretre stood silently next to her and turned his attention first to the signal of the British officers and then down along the streets where they must pass through on their long journey out of Belgium and into Holland.

Chapter Fourteen

"This is the first time that I've been out of Brussels since the German occupation. It's frightening to see how much can be destroyed in only five months," Sister White said, when they passed a village that now was only separate piles of mortar, wood, and stone where cottages once stood.

Louis Pretre pulled on his long yellow mustache.

"The journey to Louvain, which makes up only the first part of the escape route, will be relatively easy," he said, trying to reassure her.

Boger and Meachin remained quiet.

The four of them moved cautiously as if each step were a matter of life or death. If a twig broke under their feet they froze hoping no German patrols were near enough to hear. They hiked through the brush staying clear of the road. As the journey progressed Meachin remarked that escape just might be possible. Then the weariness set in. After a three hours walk they came upon a hamlet.

"I visited here once. The train switched tracks at this point," Sister White noted. "It will be a good spot to rest and change the sergeant's dressing."

Meachin rubbed his sore leg.

All that remained of the hamlet was the now familiar sight of the shelled remains of homes with piles of stone and red roof tiles. At the railroad crossing the station sat surrounded by dying grass and brambles. The termination of human maintenance was evident since the Germans closed the railway lines. A blue enameled sign post with the white letters that once pointed the way to Brussels stood with blackened ash from a shell explosion covering the words and distance. Louis stopped abruptly and whispered, "*Les casques à pointe.*"

Through the brush they saw the spiked helmets of German soldiers marching towards Brussels.

"Do you think they are searching for us?" Meachin whispered.

The Germans continued their march and soon disappeared amongst the dust clouds that were left in their wake. A little further on they came to a moss- covered barn and Louis spoke. "Here's as good a place as any. Perhaps we should rest now and sister can attend the captain's wound. It will be getting light soon. We will wait until dark and set out again."

Exhaustion gave way to sleep. It was the sound of a shell exploding that woke them all at the same instant. Another one went off and then every twenty minutes came a new explosion. Boger spoke first, "We seem to have put ourselves in the middle of a shell zone." He no sooner spoke then twelve stray shells exploded.

"Why would they be shelling here?" Meachin questioned. "The Germans sacked Louvain and the surrounding area in August. There's nothing left but burned out buildings and empty streets."

"It's the German way of keeping fear in our hearts," Louis explained.

Boger stood. "We have as much chance of being hit here by a stray shell as we do on the march. I say we leave now. No German patrols will be coming this way for a while. At least not until the shelling stops."

"I agree," Sister White added. She too rose from the ground and gathered up the bandages she took from Boger's leg.

Meachin added his comment, "If I'm going to be killed let it be while I am moving out of this God forsaken land and not cowering under some straw in a barn."

Louis Pretre rose in agreement and while another shell whistled overhead they left the sanctuary of the barn and moved on with weary, anxious steps.

Chapter Fifteen

*E*dith awoke after midnight in her chair. It was the time she would normally be preparing food for the Englishmen. She rose exhausted and went to the bed hoping to get her first night of sleep in months. With the Rappard boy safely in Holland and the captain and sergeant now on their way her work had been completed. The only worry that haunted her, other than for the safety of the four travelling across the frontier, was that she made Sister White leave.

"Should I have let her go?" she whispered aloud in a half sleep. Just before awaking she had a dream. Boger and Meachin along with Sister White were seated on a train with London markings on the front. Louis Pretre along with Doctor Depage were the engineers. She saw herself in a tower watching it all. An announcement came that the train was about to depart. She saw Francois running from the platform and Marie Depage at the ticket counter staring at the train, its wheels moving slowly, grinding on the metal rails. Madame Depage held a ticket in her hand, but her face showed an expression of dismay aware that she would not make the train on time. Francois was still running. A puff of smoke came from the engine and a gust of wind blew the steam vapor around Francois and then Marie Depage and they disappeared. Edith awoke with a shudder and the feeling that she was cold. The sound of the train whistle, shrill and piercing, still clung in her dreamy memory. She took a glass of water from the night stand and fell back to a fitful sleep.

A bright ray of sunlight woke her and she felt she had been asleep for days. She got out of bed slowly and drew the curtains. The routine of having her tea and toast brought up to her room had ended with the evacuation of her British and French nurses. The German women who replaced them were not allowed near her in private, only in the classroom or on making rounds in the Institute.

Edith brushed back her hair tightly and drew it into a bun. She looked in the mirror and her reflection seemed already to have aged beyond her forty-nine years. She stared at herself a moment thinking that she always seemed to have an old face, even as a girl. She knelt and said a prayer for Sister White, Boger, Meachin, and Louis Pretre.

It was with them in her mind that she went down the Rue de la Culture towards the market square. Since the war and the occupation the market area bore only a slight resemblance to what it once was. Gone were the live chicken peddlers. Their caged carts pulled by a team of dogs once added a certain sound to the market: a mixture of cart wheels rumbling across gravel, dogs murmuring in their muzzles, and chickens cackling in their wooden cages. Gone too were the fish dealers and vegetable peddlers. In these days of German occupation all goods and produce were purchased on the sly and there was always the threat of the Germans getting wind of food supplies being kept from their use. She had to take the risk and moved closer to the man whom she came to see. Monsieur Givency directed a nod and wink her way when he noticed her approaching.

"I have nothing, Madame Cavell," he said, dispirited.

Givency arranged a row of wicker baskets on a cart.

Edith looked around the nearly empty square.

"Some cabbages, cheese, butter?"

"All gone. The Germans discovered my supplier last evening. Everything is on its way to the front and he is being sent to a work camp."

Edith let out a long sigh.

The peddler was in a mood to talk. "I have had just about enough of these invaders," Givency bit on the stem of his unlit pipe. I'm going to do something."

"It can't go on like this forever," Edith tried to be reassuring.

Givency, approaching seventy, found it hard to adjust. "I remember the way it used to be."

"We all do."

"No. I mean years ago. My family lived in Upper Belgium. Just south of the Sambre and the Meuse at the Condroz plateau. We had a cattle ranch—"

Edith grabbed his arm to silence him when a small patrol of Germans came around the corner.

"Be patient, my friend, God will help us."

"I'm going to do something."

Edith found it hard to get Givency out of her mind after returning to Berkendael. The old man's watery eyes and shaking hands stayed with her as she hung up her coat and was about to begin work on her next day's lecture.

A knock on her door momentarily startled her.

"Yes."

"You are needed downstairs, Matron Cavell," the attempt at French with the trace of a German accent let her know it was Anna, a girl of eighteen who seemed different than the other German nurses. Anna, an orphan from Bavaria, seemed to look at Edith with a respect and admiration as if they were related. It was always the young who saw through the divisions of War, Edith considered, thinking that in other times Anna would be a good match for Francois.

"I shall be there in a moment, Anna, thank you."

Edith listened to the footsteps go down the hall. She took her bible and sat to pray one last prayer before starting her day.

There was a confusion of nurses and soldiers at the entrance to the surgical house. With the beds now almost all taken since the wounded came from Ypres Edith wondered if more were coming and where would she put them?

General von Bissing himself stood in the midst of the assemblage of soldiers shouting orders at a rapid pace. Edith could not make out what he was saying, the little German she knew could not keep up with the quickness of his speech. Edith noticed Anna at the outer circle of the group and waived her over when their eyes met. In acknowledgement of the fact that Anna seemed different than the rest and in keeping with the bond that seemed to be growing between them Edith chose to speak in French. Anna seemed pleased at the gesture.

"Who is it that wanted to see me?"

"General von Bissing."

"Well, he seems occupied at the moment."

"Another *Francs-Tireurs*," Anna explained, with a concerned look.

"Who did the sniper shoot at?"

"One of von Bissing's adjutants. The man is being brought here."

"Where did it happen?"

"In the market square."

"Have a bed prepared. Also, see if you can locate Doctor Depage. I would like a word with him."

"He is gone."

"Gone? Gone where?"

Anna shrugged her shoulders. The commotion seemed to be lessening. A stretcher was being carried in.

"Go to your ward, Sister. I will be along shortly."

Anna left quickly. Edith called out to her, "When did Doctor Depage leave? Did he say when he would return?"

Anna didn't hear. Edith approached von Bissing.

Von Bissing continued to give orders, but in reverence for the stretcher on which his aide lay, the General lowered his tone. When he noticed Edith he aggressively tugged on the lapels of his opened coat and pushed through the crowd. He signaled for one of his lieutenants.

"I have sent your Doctor Depage away. I will assume control here."

"Where?"

"To Ghent. He will be in the service of the Fourth Army. They need trained medical help there and that will be his job."

"He did not mention anything to me."

von Bissing acted as if he didn't hear. He went on, "Also, with this

Francs-Tireurs business I cannot take chances. His employee has been found guilty of an attack on Sergeant Uber. I cannot have collaborators here or anywhere else in Belgium."

"Employee? Who?"

"The sniper is named Francois Guton."

"Francois? He is only a child and Doctor Depage is certainly not a collaborator, General."

"I shoot collaborators, Madame Cavell," von Bissing looked directly into Edith's eyes and for a moment she thought that she would be arrested.

"We are all aware of the policy towards collaborators," she found the courage to say.

"You will see to my adjutant personally. Meanwhile I want to check on Sergeant Uber."

"Certainly. I will take you to him," Edith said, without expression, waiting for the right moment to plead for the release of Francois."

Two nurses were at Sergeant Uber's bedside. One of them spoke, "He has developed a fever. We fear of an infection."

"You can finish your rounds, sisters, I will tend to the sergeant," Edith said, taking a cool towel and placing it on Uber's forehead.

Uber opened his eyes aware of the gentle treatment Edith was giving him, a German who had occupied her country.

"You will be fine, sergeant," Edith whispered, while changing his bandages. There is no infection."

"*Danke schön*," Uber said, raising his head slightly from the pillow and noticing von Bissing speaking with an aide.

"Why is he here?" Uber asked, softly in French.

Seeing Edith's surprise he explained almost apologetically, "my mother is French." Uber put his finger to his lips, "Our secret, Madame."

"Yes, our secret," Edith agreed, while reaching for a basin of water. She began to wash Uber's back.

At that moment von Bissing's adjutant was carried in and placed in the bed next to Uber. The man was conscious and talking quickly. He too, as did Uber, only received a minor wound.

von Bissing watched as Edith went about her work.

"As a career officer I have witnessed many medical procedures both in civilian and army field hospitals. Very professional, Miss Cavell," von Bissing said. "After the war I will bring you to Berlin to train nurses, Miss Cavell."

Edith didn't answer. She took a thermometer and inserted it under Uber's tongue.

"The peddler of wicker baskets was shot. Did you know him?"

Again Edith didn't answer. She prayed silently for Givency's soul and had to tighten her eyes shut so as not to shed tears. There would be time for that later in her room.

von Bissing moved to leave. Edith washed her hands in a basin and dried them hastily, intending to follow the general and request that he intercede on behalf of Francois.

von Bissing reached the door and turned.

"Where would you like it?"

"Excuse me, General."

"The other body. Two attacks on German soldiers cannot be cancelled by the death of only one peddler. Where do you want it?"

"Which body?"

"The *Franc-Tireurs*."

Edith stood silent trying to decipher his words.

"The body of Depage's collaborator. He was shot at dawn. All collaborators are shot. I told you that, Miss Cavell. Three more will have to pay the price for this last sniper attack. I will take the first three men I see when I leave here."

Edith couldn't bear to be present when they brought the body of Francois back to Berkendael. Seeing him, lifeless and cold, seemed to be the end of not only his life but of all innocence. She took out her bible, but put it down. With Depage sent away and Marie out of the country there was no one left to assume the responsibility for Francois. She straightened the photograph of her father and went to await the soldiers who were returning Francois to his home.

Rain pelted the window of her room leaving tiny droplets clinging to the glass. The drops hung there for a moment and then trickled down the window to disappear. Edith thought that a poet might liken the rain to tears, yet she couldn't. There was nothing poetic in this war.

She found that the most melancholy time for her was the dinner hour. It was at that time that the memories of Swardeston seemed most alive: the carrying of meals to the poor of the village; her father saying grace and reminding her of her obligation to serve those in need; her wish to grow up like other girls and marry and raise children and the conviction in her heart, even then, that that would never be. Swardeston was all of those things to her.

She rubbed her hands across her face and the dark, foggy streets of Swardeston were alive. She could hear her footsteps on the cobbles. She gently pushed aside her drapes and watched another German patrol on its rounds. Perhaps one of them shot Francois. The boy's fate was now sealed for eternity, his life ended, but the fate of Doctor Depage, of Marie, of Sister White, of Boger and Meachin, of even herself lay in question. She pulled up a chair and sat looking into the obscurity of the dark Belgian night wondering when and where it would all end.

Chapter Sixteen

"*I*t was the right decision to have Francois buried on the grounds of Berkendael," Father Gilbert said, blessing the soil.

"If the French, Belgians, and British win this war he will be on home soil and if the German's prove victorious Francois' grave will be a silent witness to how they achieved their ends," Edith answered, without taking her eyes from the newly dug grave.

A light snow began falling, the cold wet flakes dropping on Edith's face like tears. With the snow came a bitter, cold wind. She, followed by Father Gilbert, made up the funeral procession which accompanied the body to the point on the Berkendael grounds which lay farthest from the road. The plot was set aside for Doctor Depage when the time came. Edith always thought that he or Marie, or perhaps even herself, would be the first to lay here, but certainly not one as young as Francois.

The gravedigger lowered the body into the hole, the priest said a few hasty words, looking over his shoulder lest a German might see him and add to his already precarious position in this occupied city. He flung a handful of dirt on the grave and a splash of holy water accompanied by a quick prayer in Latin. He nodded to the gravedigger to cover the hole and bowed to Edith as he made his retreat from the grave.

Edith stood silent, considering just how she would eventually tell the Doctor and Madame Depage about the boy's murder. She felt a light tapping on her shoulder. At first she thought it to be the heavier flakes of snow which were falling at an accelerated rate. The tapping came again and she turned to see the gravedigger. He lifted the faded corduroy cap he wore low over his eyes and Edith recognized at once, even under the dirt and grime, the face of Herman Capiau.

"Monsieur Capiau."

Capiau gently tugged her elbow indicating he wanted her to accompany him inside the institute.

Edith brought Capiau in through the cellar door. She closed and bolted it, drawing closed a tiny lace curtain over the window cut into the door. They walked quietly under the low beams, brushing away cobwebs as they went. A hole in one of the shutters allowed a bit of light in through the iron-grilled window.

Underneath the window stood a small table with an empty stone crock that once held a small amount of patè and sausage for Boger and Meachin. A wicker basket sat like an invited guest. It was where Francois kept his mud boots after completing his gardening chores.

Capiau looked at Edith with patient eyes waiting for her to deem it safe to speak. She listened for any sounds and then nodded to Herman that they could talk.

"We have had word, some good some not," Capiau began.

Edith straightened herself as if to prepare for a blow.

Capiau continued, "Louis Pretre found it necessary to change plans somewhat and had to separate earlier than planned. Pretre used a Belgian who smuggles newspapers into Holland as a guide for Sergeant Meachin. They reached the border and are safely in Holland."

"And the others?" Edith asked, calmly.

"Sister White crossed the frontier and is on her way to London with all of the papers she is carrying. Captain Boger, however, has been recaptured and sent to a POW camp at Ruhleben. I'm afraid there is nothing we can do for him now and he will wait out the war there. Still, he is alive and that is something."

"Yes. I appreciate your risk in bringing me this news. Can I give you some food for your journey back to Wasmes?"

"No, there is a more important reason for my coming here today, Miss Cavell."

"Yes."

"I have been reporting your successes to de Croy. First with the Rappard boy and now with the two British officers. We need to ask a very large request of you. As you know we have been combing the fields around Mons for soldiers separated from their units. Now we have extended that to cover the area from Mons north to the coast and south to Charlerol. We have many in need of our help and we need a place to hide them until we can get them out of Belgium."

"I have helped three people, Mr. Capiau, and I have no regrets, but now the Germans are completely in control here. Depage has been sent to Ghent. Sister White and my nurses are gone. It would be too much of a risk for anyone to stay here."

"No more of a risk than where they are now, lost and cut off on the Western Front. These allied soldiers will be shot if found by the Germans."

"I understand that, but to bring them here?"

"We have just enlisted a new man," Capiau began to explain, thinking of his own reservations about Phillipe Baucq, "he is an architect who lives here in Brussels. We will be able to move the soldiers we place here out much quicker. Baucq can keep track of the German patrol movements. We will use his home as a safe house and he can help in coordinating escape plans and securing guides."

"It will be more difficult to move soldiers in and out now that von Bissing has taken control of Berkendael. And now I will be working alone."

Capiau offered no response. Edith spoke correctly in her statements. He was about to agree and be on his way when Edith touched his arm. "I will do what I can," Edith said, thinking about those days back in Swardeston and the food she brought to the poor. She remembered the last time she saw Francois alive and the cold snow that now covered his buried body. "Give me a week before you send anyone here."

"I can find no words to thank you, Miss Cavell," Capiau said, kissing her hand. He pulled up his collar and moved toward the door and out into the shadows of the Berkendael courtyard.

Chapter Seventeen

*E*dith, sitting at her writing desk, heard a commotion coming from the hall. It disturbed her thoughts. A nurse, in the German accented French she became accustomed to lately, knocked and began speaking before the door could be opened.

"Matron Cavell, we need your assistance. There is a problem."

"Yes, I am coming," Edith answered, rising from her chair.

When she opened the door the nurse who had been summoning her was already on her way down the hall towards the source of the commotion. An older woman, speaking in fragmented sentences that were full of worry, stood in the middle of a group of nurses. The woman went back and forth between French and Flemish, not seeming to realize that only German would be understood by the majority of women standing before her.

One of the nurses turned to Edith as she approached and said, "I think she is saying something about a wounded child. She wants us to send someone. I told her to try a private doctor we only treat German soldiers here."

It was all Edith could do to keep from pushing her away. "Thank you, Sister. I will deal with this. You can all return to your duties."

The group of nurses scattered quickly, relieved to be rid of the annoying Belgian woman. One of them spoke and obviously wanted Edith to hear because she spoke in French, "A defeated civilian has no place in a German occupied land, even if that land was once hers."

Edith disregarded the comment and turned her attention to the distraught woman.

"It is my son, Madame," the woman said, tugging nervously on her kerchief.

Edith took her gently by the arm. "Come into my office. I have some tea and you can explain to me what happened." Even as she said the words Edith wondered how she would tell this woman, this fellow countryman, that the insensitive German nurses were indeed correct: only Germans could be treated.

Edith closed the door, still mentally choosing her words, knowing that no matter what she said it would amount to a poor explanation. The woman took off her tattered mauve kerchief and straightened her body from the stooped posture she appeared to have.

"Capiau sends his regards," she said, "four British soldiers will be arriving in the morning."

Edith recovered quickly from her surprise.

"Four?"

"Just the beginning I'm afraid. I also have news. Sister White reached London in time for New Years punch with the Prime Minister."

"And mother?"

"I'm sorry, Miss Cavell, she passed on."

Edith closed her eyes and lowered her head. She composed herself. "Did she receive my letter?"

"Yes. She passed away the next morning. Your letter was on her pillow."

Without any further words the woman pushed her hair under the kerchief and assumed her stoop. She opened the door. In a loud voice she said, "Why can no one help? Just because I am not German." The woman, now a distraught mother again, raced out of the institute and into the Brussels twilight. Edith knelt and prayed for her mothers' soul. She thought: life can change so abruptly. Now I must go on alone, in a new direction than the one I planned when I first left England. A simple knock on the door brought the Rappard boy to her; another knock and Herman Capiau appeared with Boger and Meachin; now the escape mechanism of de Croy again turned her way.

Just before dawn a cart pulled up to the Institute and four Belgian laborers, silent and uneasy, slowly stepped from the surrey, their heads bowed. They made for the side entrance that led to the basement. Edith stood waiting with warm blankets and a plate of sausage and bread. Without a word she handed each man a blanket pointing in the direction of the east wall where a small door led to a crawl space that would be their home for as long as it took to safely transport them to Holland.

By 7:00 AM she was at her lecture podium in the sisters' hall for a talk on the proper techniques for the disinfecting of wounds. By 8:00 AM she was at her desk recording her official records of food costs and expenses. Then it was a long day of administrative duties and patient care. It was the same duties she performed countless times, but now she felt a stranger in this Institute she called home and it was only her work that seemed to be real. Doctor Depage gone, Marie away, Francois murdered; the sisters' chattering in German; the thud of jackboots in the hallway; the intermittent inspections by taciturn German officers; all of it made for a nightmare vision of reality. The days were long waiting games for when her real work began: caring for any Allied soldiers she was harboring. There was no one to confer with on the needs of the men hidden in attics and crawlspaces, unused rooms, or garden sheds. Their welfare fell to her and her alone. The nights were taken up in preparation of whatever food she could find for them.

The hours between midnight and dawn were set aside for finding guides, clothes, or to maintain contact with Capiau and de Croy through the messages she left in or retrieved from Phillipe Baucq's postal box. Tonight there was a note that another "visitor" would be stopping to see her. Also the meeting she requested had been arranged. She put another log on the fire and prepared to wait until it was safe to leave. The floorboards were cold. She rubbed her arms and knees for warmth. The suddenness of the winter cold fell on Brussels and the reality of those heat filled August days of German occupation became secondary on people's minds. Why it happened and how it happened were questions that no longer held any relevance to the citizens of Belgium. It did happen and now we must live with it was the sentiment that mattered. And more importantly surviving the cold winter with less than was needed became the priority. All raw materials, goods, and products fell into the bottomless pit that comprised the German war machine. Edith buttoned her coat and tied a scarf around her head while she made a mental note of what she would tall Capiau. The meeting was hastily arranged at the home of Phillipe Baucq.

Edith looked at her clock. Two in the morning. She peeked through the iced window panes into the deserted street. At any moment a German patrol could pass by, but she knew she had to risk it. The Allied soldiers she would be aiding would not make it across the frontier into Holland unless they had woolen clothes, blankets, boots, sweaters, overcoats, to say nothing of the food.

Edith felt the sting of the cold on her cheeks. She moved along the Rue de la Culture stiff from the chill and going over in her mind the excuses she would give to any German who happened to stop her. I am a nurse and I am needed at so and so's home. I have been called away from Berkendael to attend to one of the surgical hospitals on the outskirts of town. As she approached Baucq's home she was relieved that she didn't meet any patrols. A quick knock and the side door opened. Phillipe stood in his dressing gown.

"Capiau has not arrived yet," Baucq said, closing the door quickly as soon as Edith entered.

"Has he sent any word?"

"No."

Edith took off her kerchief and shook the cold air from the folds. She took out a pen and paper and began to write the items she needed.

"I have a fire lit in the sitting room."

Edith followed him in. The room, warm and decorated in an old style with furnishings that obviously were in the Baucq family for generations, reminded Edith of what Belgium was like before the war, before the Germans.

"I will leave you a moment while I dress," Phillipe announced.

Edith nodded and sat close to the fire. By instinct she took out the prayer book she always carried. The lessons learned at Swardeston had been set as if in cement. She opened to one of her favorites, the Third Collect:

Lighten our darkness,
we beseech thee, O Lord;
and by thy great mercy
defend us from all perils and
dangers of this night;
for the love of thy only Son,
our Savior, Jesus Christ. Amen.

Phillipe entered the room with a grave expression on his face and a note in his hand.

"Capiau sent word," Baucq said. "Too dangerous to leave Wasmes. I'll be taking the list of things you require to him in the morning."

Edith put away the prayer book.

"Coffee, Miss Cavell?"

"No, I must get back. Tell Capiau anything at all he can bring will help. I have a guide ready for next week to bring some of the men into Holland."

"Have faith, Miss Cavell. We will do our best."

"I have faith. I need woolen clothing."

Edith wrapped the kerchief around her hair and felt the pain in her lungs as she breathed in the icy air.

When she arrived back at the Institute it was 4:00 AM. A scared French lieutenant was hiding in the alley.

"You must be the visitor I've been told to expect."

"I don't feel like a visitor, Madame," the man managed a weak and frightened smile.

She placed him in a bed next to a severely wounded German sergeant and forged the papers that listed the Frenchman as a shell shocked German infantryman just arrived from the trenches.

Dawn arrived and Edith awoke to the sounds of a German patrol receiving their orders in the avenue outside the Institute. She believed it to be the search of Berkendael she had been fearing. She buttoned her collar hastily wondering if they had not already found the four British soldiers in the basement and the French one in the surgical house recovery area. Had she forged his papers well enough? she wondered. Did she leave some clue, perhaps a bit of cooked meat, or a dirty plate overlooked? The late hours and little sleep were taking a toll on her nerves. She knew that. Still there was no room for mistakes. She went to the door. A knock came as she reached it and she opened the door slowly expecting for the room to be rushed by German soldiers and that she would be arrested. The hallway was silent. Sergeant Uber stood alone at the door.

"I hope I did not wake you, Matron."

"No," Edith answered, her words choked by apprehension and fear.

"My captain has come for me and I wanted to thank you before I left," Uber said, looking over his shoulder at the stairs. "I shouldn't want to be found here. You understand."

"Yes. But there is no need for thanks. I was simply doing my job."

"Perhaps, but a citizen of an occupied country treating a soldier from the other side…well, I will not forget it." Uber turned and was gone. Edith stood for a moment at the door. She was slowly closing it when she smelled smoke and followed it down the stairs where Uber had just went.

Outside a patrol was scattering in all directions up and down the avenue. Uber was still on the steps strapping on his revolver. He spoke to her out of the corner of his mouth so no one would see him conversing with the enemy.

"Another *Franc-Tireurs* attack."

"When?"

"This morning. A sniper killed a sentry at von Bissing's headquarters."

"What are they doing now?" Edith asked, peering at the smoke coming from a row of houses south of the Institute.

"They have set fires and are waiting for the inhabitants to come out. Our orders are to shoot as many Belgians as we find. I am sorry, Madame," Uber rushed into the street his revolver drawn. He looked back for a quick glance at Edith and she noticed the wetness around his eyes and the tightness of his lips. A door opened in one of the houses and Edith turned away quickly just as the shots went off.

Chapter Eighteen

*F*ebruary ended with bitter cold weather. The threat of a heavy winter storm hung ominously in the gray skies and dark clouds. Belgium had become familiar with living under the threat of storm. A prayer for an early spring was muttered in passing by all who passed a church, chapel, or synagogue. Edith warmed her hands over the fire. She tried to compose a note that she would send to Capiau:

This country has been progressively harvested for goods and raw materials that can be supplied to the German soldiers and it is impossible to find woolen clothes, overcoats, sweaters, blankets or boots. We will not be able to send anyone to Holland unless we can prepare them against the cold.

Edith read the note and then crumbled it and tossed it into the fire. I must see him in person, she thought. It was as the paper burned that she remembered Marguerite Graux. She grabbed her coat and shawl and within moments was on the Rue du Canal Vaarstratt. A chambermaid opened the door.

"Madame Graux is hosting a dinner party. I cannot disturb her."

Edith took out an envelope and wrote on the back of it. "Please give her this. I will wait."

The maid begrudgingly took the note and sighed as if it would do no good, but she would see the Madame received it. She closed the door without a word. Twenty minutes later the door opened again. Edith shivered and took her shawl from her mouth. "Yes."

The maid handed her the envelope Edith gave her earlier, nodded her head politely and closed the door. Edith was about to toss the envelope away and leave when she noticed the envelope was thicker. She moved into the light of a lamp. Underneath Edith's note Marguerite wrote:

> *Forgive me for not wanting to implicate myself, but I hope this will help. See the merchant Pollard at the end of this Avenue.*

Edith opened the envelope and took out the money Marguerite put there. She hurried down the Rue du Canal Vaarstratt to the shop of the tailor Monsieur Pollard.

The four British soldiers that Capiau sent in January, along with the lone Frenchman, and six Canadians that arrived in the first week of February, were able to be moved out successfully thanks to Marguerite Graux and the tailor Pollard. Phillipe Baucq proved useful in getting them on their way, but Edith found herself checking on the man a number of times in order to make sure all documents were dated properly and that reliable guides were secured for the journeys on various routes across the Belgian frontier into Holland. As it was, Baucq forgot the identity cards in his flat and had to back track to get them costing a four hour delay of the escape. Phillipe Baucq although patriotic, courageous, and compassionate, was also forgetful, disorganized, and hasty. Edith harbored a worried concern for his continuing role in the escape organization as she went through the basement of Berkendael and removed any traces of the soldiers who hid there. A discarded crumb of bread, a thread caught on a chair, a scrap of an intended letter home to England. She waited a moment at the door that led upstairs and composed herself, satisfied that it was safe to go to her room. She stopped at the front door to pull down the shade and noticed the empty envelope that lay on the floor near the letter slot. The blank red paper inside was a signal that more soldiers would be arriving within the next day or two.

Edith barely slept and all the next day she wondered when and how many soldiers would be arriving. Early afternoon brought a cart carrying three Belgian laborers with orders that they were to repair one of the German ammunition wagons. Edith looked at the man who handed her the papers, not forged very well.

He whispered the name 'Capiau' and she ushered them inside and into the basement.

March brought an average of three soldiers every eight days to Berkendael. Edith carried on with her regular duties of supervising the sisters and made sure that her daily lectures continued uninterrupted. She gleaned information from the German nurses, most of whom had soldiers as boyfriends. Snippets of information concerning troop movements gleaned when a boyfriend was being transferred and where he was going to send his letters from were meticulously noted and relayed to Capiau.

Food allowances were being reduced and occupied Belgian continued to be looked at as a storehouse for the German infantry. Edith managed to feed not only her patients and staff, but also all hidden soldiers. No area of Berkendael, whether it be attic, basement, or crawlspace went without at some point hiding an escaping Allied soldier.

By late March Edith was forced to place some of the Allied soldiers in the ward amongst German soldiers. Their reports always said they were shell-shocked or mortally wounded and no one asked any questions.

More German nurses were being brought in. All British and French sisters were sent home, which left only one Belgian woman and Edith of the original staff brought in by Doctor Depage. Before Sister White left she mentioned her thoughts about this woman. The Belgian sister, a woman named Helen Rosset, couldn't be trusted. She had been seen in the taverns with various German soldiers and recently had become the mistress of a Prussian captain. Edith remembered Sister White's words of caution when she noticed Sister Helen checking the charts of the allied soldiers who were disguised as wounded German infantrymen.

Chapter Nineteen

"Why have I been brought here?" Edith asked quietly, fearing that she already knew the answer.

General von Bissing looked at her through his monocle like she were an annoying child who doesn't need or deserve a response.

"I will attend to you in a moment, Miss Cavell," von Bissing said, in a serious tone, but something in his eyes and his manner seemed to suggest that he still had not formulated an opinion of her. It allowed Edith a small sense of relief.

von Bissing continued talking in hushed tones to two of his officers. He then dismissed them and let the monocle fall from his eye and dangle on its cord.

Edith felt as if she too was being treated in the same way and she wondered just how long she would be kept hanging by suspicion. How much did von Bissing know?

"There are certain sectors of the Front where we suspect that Allied soldiers, defeated Allied soldiers, are being aided to escape."

Edith stared at him blankly. She couldn't get out of her mind the way he told her that Francois had been executed.

von Bissing continued, "We have cut off a few English battalions, or what is left of them, and yet we cannot account for some of the soldiers."

"I hear that the shells of your howitzers can destroy all traces of a man," Edith answered, coldly.

"Yes, that is true," von Bissing said, taking her comment as a tribute, "but we are not that accurate. No. I believe that a group of Belgians are giving aid to the enemy."

"To your enemy, sir, not ours."

The muscles in von Bissing's cheek pulsed and the veins in his neck stood out. He forced himself to remain calm.

"Since Belgium is in our control and I am the governor-general I will tell you who your enemies are and who they are not."

Edith didn't respond. From here on in she knew that the less she said the better.

von Bissing eased to the window, crossing the thick piled red carpet with slow deliberate steps. He nonchalantly drew the curtains as if he were alone. With his back to Edith he spoke. "We will find those responsible for aiding the Allies."

"Yes, there is that possibility."

von Bissing swung his body around to face Edith.

"No, not a possibility. It is a fact. We will find them and it is the Belgian people who will be held accountable."

"As they have been held accountable for each sniper attack?" Edith answered calmly, thinking of Francois.

"Yes. *Franc-Tireurs* are Belgians and it is Belgians who must answer for their actions, just as they must answer for anyone aiding the Allies."

"I still do not know how that involves me and why I have been brought here."

"I am aware of your, how shall I say, sympathies. You are English with strong ties here in Belgium. If you know anything you must tell me now or pay the consequences."

"As Francois did?"

"Yes." von Bissing's voice showed only coldness.

"It is war, Miss Cavell," he added.

"I do not know anything."

von Bissing took a moment to respond.

"Collaborators are to be shot, Miss Cavell. I have already told you that. I shall be watching you closely."

"Am I free to go?"

von Bissing turned to the window and answered, "Yes. For now, Miss Cavell. For now."

Chapter Twenty

$\mathcal{E}$dith sensed something to be wrong from the hastily written note that came concealed in a box of medical bandages. The note, signed by P.B., meant that Baucq wanted to see her. A time of 1:00 A.M. for the next day of April 25, 1915 was scrawled in the margin.

The sense of foreboding she felt about the note from Phillipe Baucq was confirmed when she arrived at the basement room in the Baucq home. One look at the expressions of Capiau and Baucq's faces told it all. There was trouble.

"Thank you for coming, Miss Cavell," Capiau said, ushering her to a seat at the table lit by a small oil lamp.

In the half-light Edith noticed de Croy going over some papers in the corner. The others were apparently waiting for him to take a seat at the table. de Croy remained in the shadow of the corner and spoke, "The news from Ypres is not good. The Germans have begun another attack on the city in an attempt to push through the British and Belgian front lines and take Calais."

"When?" someone asked.

"Thursday, the 22nd. The fighting is still going on."

"The Allies have been making progress. They've held back the Germans at Ypres before. They can do it again." The voice of a man Edith did not recognize.

de Croy's face seemed almost ghostlike. "This time it is different. I have an eyewitness account from a soldier we found last night."

"And?" Capiau asked.

"From what we could gather from this man, who was shell-shocked, on the evening of the twenty-second the soldiers in the French front line trenches took the worst of it. He told us that a rising cloud of a green vapor came from shells fired from the advanced German lines. The vapor settled on the ground like mist and drifted towards the French trenches on a brisk wind. At first the soldiers became nauseous, then they fainted and collapsed."

"How many casualties?"

"We don't know that yet. The Germans, wearing some type of mask, charged in behind the vapor and met no resistance from the paralyzed French front. They were spraying more gas as they advanced. Some of the soldiers have already died."

"Have the Germans occupied the front line trenches?"

"Yes. Any of those that might have escaped are wandering now, half blinded by the gas with the worst affects still to come once it reaches their lungs. We have to find as many of the French soldiers as we can. That is why I have asked you here. We need to work fast." de Croy turned to Edith, "I expect that we will have many for you, Miss Cavell. Also, I have information about Berkendael. There is an informer."

Edith moved down the Rue de la Culture uneasily, as if for the first time. Someone she knew, someone she may have passed every day, perhaps someone she once treated at Berkendael, was informing on her comings and goings. The thought unsettled her, but the fact remained. de Croy made a point of letting her read the copy of the German surveillance report he got his hands on. No names were mentioned except for the words "our source", typed above the paragraph which noted a procession of men who passed through the doors of the Institute. It may have been for money, for food, or simply for warm clothes and blankets, but a citizen of Brussels was collaborating with the Germans. She could feel the impending hand on the shoulder, she could hear the words that would be spoken, probably in poor French with a German accent: "Stop! You are under arrest." Edith felt in her heart that it was only a matter of time before she would be taken prisoner. Nothing could alter the course she chose, and she felt no compunction to alter it. She would do what she must do. Had not the Vicar instilled that in her? She looked into the eastern sky towards Holland. She did right to get so many across its borders, but there would be no one to take her to safety. A tap on her shoulder took her from her thoughts. Capiau himself brought a wounded soldier, a British Lieutenant-Colonel. Herman whispered, "The man's rank demanded a reliable guide to bring him here. I didn't want to take any chances. He knows too many details about French and British troop movements."

Capiau didn't have to say that if this man were captured he would most assuredly be tortured. Edith looked in the Lieutenant-Colonel's eyes. They were glassy and he was barely conscious.

"His name is John Dickenson and he is a victim of the gas attack at Ypres. He also has a leg wound, not a serious one, but one that can turn gangrenous if not treated."

"I will take him from here. You'd better go," Edith said, easing the wounded man into the alley and in the side door. Capiau disappeared without a word.

Chapter Twenty-One

A hard rain fell on the first of May. Someone left a window open in the hall and Edith slipped on the wet rain soaked floor. The dressings and bandages she kept hidden under her skirt scattered across the carpet. A German officer on the landing began approaching her direction while looking over a clipboard. Being preoccupied he hadn't yet seen her trying to retrieve the scattered medical supplies.

Sister Anna came from her room and, although not knowing what was happening, she sensed something to be wrong from the way Edith nervously picked up the supplies while constantly checking on the location of the approaching German officer.

"Didn't I see you on the Avenue yesterday. You helped me with some packages?" Anna flirted with one eye on Edith who desperately reached for the scattered bandages.

"I think I would have remembered you," the officer took the bait and stopped to talk.

It gave Edith enough time to gather the rest of the medical supplies. Straightening her skirt she passed the couple.

"Come, Sister Anna, the lecture."

Anna left the officer in his frustration.

When they reached the end of the hall Edith attempted to begin an explanation.

Anna put up a hand. "I have no need to know anything, Matron

Cavell," she said, and went down the steps to the nurses' hall.

It had been a long, tedious, and anxious day in the wards. She was apprehensive about Lieutenant-Colonel Dickenson. His leg needed a change of bandages, but she had been prevented from attending to him. The Germans twice searched Berkendael and special attention was paid to Edith's office and rooms although the searching officers tried to disguise their interest in her by checking all the rooms. She knew she had been careful and left no traces of incriminating evidence, still a search was unnerving.

The midnight bells rang. Berkendael was very quiet. The rain added a melancholy air to the halls and she recalled other days when she and Marie would have shared a hot cocoa on just such a night. When she reached Lieutenant-Colonel Dickenson he was sitting on his cot, removing all of his bandages and attempting to apply a field dressing taken from his service kit.

"I'm pleased to find you conscious, but you shouldn't be doing that," Edith announced in a whisper, taking the gauze from his hands and preparing one of her own.

"I was a bit out of it the last time we met, Miss Cavell. I do apologize. How long have I been here?"

"Almost three days."

"Three Days! I have to get back."

"The war is over for you. You're staying here in Brussels until you can be safely moved to Holland."

"My men."

"They will continue without you."

"What's left of them," Dickenson said, falling back onto the cot. "I can still see them; their dazed eyes and white faces from the months in those muddy trenches."

"The battle didn't go well I'm told."

"It was the damn gas. I'm with the 46th North Midland Division and my battalion held a perilous section of the Ypres Salient. I'm afraid there were many casualties."

"There will be more before this war is over, I fear," Edith said, softly, "but you must get well now and get back to England."

"I'll get back to England, but I don't know if I'll ever be well again. They can give you morphia for the wounds, but there is no anodyne for the memories."

Edith let him sleep and quietly went back to her room. She lay on the bed and took the letter that had arrived in the morning from Madame Depage.

She saved the reading of it all through the day. She wanted to savor the fact that she wasn't alone and that Marie would soon be back. No word came from Doctor Depage and Edith knew she would have to confront Marie with that news and the news about Francois immediately upon the woman's return.

For now she took pleasure in reading the letter:

I leave New York on May 1 and my trip has been a successful one. I have done quite well in my fund raising and am traveling with a man named Alfred Vanderbilt. You may know the name. He wants to meet Antoine and see the Institute as soon as the war is ended. In the meantime he has been quite generous with a donation. I am very excited about the ship I am taking. The Lusitania is a grand ship. It is 785 feet in length and 31,550 gross tons. You know how much I enjoy details. She has captured the coveted 'Blue Riband' from the German liner Deutschland and I am proud of that. We should reach Ireland on May 7 and then I'll conclude some business in London and be back at Berkendael. With affection, Marie.

Edith placed the letter on the nightstand facing her and lay her head on the pillow. In the months since Madame Depage left Brussels the world had changed so much. She almost wished there were a way of contacting her and telling her to stay in London until the war ended. But when would that be?

Chapter Twenty-Two

*I*t was late in the morning when a man dressed in a Belgian worker's clothes began approaching Edith as she carried back the rationing of bread allotted by von Bissing's Civil Administrator. She avoided making eye contact with the man; something about his clothes, so clean, disturbed her. He followed steadily behind her getting closer with each step. He spoke in a hushed voice, in perfect French, "Please wait."

Edith purposely dropped her bags of bread assuming that the man would stop to help allowing him time to state his business without being conspicuous.

"I was given your name by a peasant family in Mons," he said, stooping to help pick up the loaves.

"I do not know anyone in Mons, Monsieur," Edith answered slowly, putting the bread into her basket while trying to size up the man beside her.

"Please, Madame, I have been in a German labor camp. I have escaped and I need your help."

Edith looked at him suspiciously. "What else did this peasant family tell you?" she asked, hoping for the password she and Capiau agreed upon should the situation arise where a soldier made it to Brussels alone without a guide from de Croy. How else would he know of me? Edith wondered, still studying the man's face.

"They told me that you are a good woman who has helped many like me."

Edith rose slowly.

"My name is Private Harold Jenkins. I was at Ypres. I need to get to Holland."

A German patrol began to enter the Avenue at its farthest point. The thoughts ran quickly through Edith's mind: he has no password, he never mentioned Capiau nor de Croy.

The German patrol drew closer, their footsteps now within ear shot. The footsteps reminded her of the day a patrol marched Francois away and to his death.

"Hurry down that alley. At the end is a fence. If you climb it you will be on Berkendael grounds. Hide in the tool shed until I can come for you."

The man smiled, pulled his cap down low over his eyes, and raced down the alley.

Lieutenant-Colonel Dickenson and the man called Jenkins left Berkendael on the same day, May 7. Edith was careful never to have the two men meet or to even learn of each other's existence. After subtly trying to inquire of Dickenson the names of the men in his regiment she became worried when she off-handedly posed the name of Private Harold Jenkins and he did not respond going so far as to say he knew of no man named Jenkins. Edith found separate guides for them and made sure that Dickenson left first.

She waited until evening to go to the attic room where she hid Jenkins to make sure that no trace of him was left. She took away the blanket she gave him. Under the bed frame she found papers, suspiciously torn into small pieces.

Edith still held the bits of paper in her hand when she entered her room and slumped into a chair. She made an attempt to piece the scraps together, but not all of the fragments were there. The rains began again and she placed a log on the fire and turned on the radio. There would only be German propaganda broadcasts, but the noise eased the silence.

A German band played march tunes. A clear voiced announcer inter-rupted: "We interrupt our musical selections tonight. The German High Command has warned through announcements in our broadcasts and newspapers that all forms of collaboration with our enemies will be dealt with severely. As a result of trying to smuggle a cargo of small arms to the allied forces the *Lusitania* was sunk by one of our U-boats, U-20. Two thousand lives were lost in an act that could have been prevented. The Fatherland shall prevail."

The music returned immediately. Edith stared at the letter from Ma-rie Depage that still sat on her night table and then buried her head in her hands. "Oh, Marie. You too are gone."

Chapter Twenty-Three

*E*dith didn't know for how long she sat there. The radio turned to static for what seemed like hours. In the hearth the wood became cold hardened charcoal and a draft from the open flue brushed against her legs. She wondered how cold might the waters off of Ireland's coast be. Two thousand lives. Marie lost.

Her eyes moved across the room while her body remained rigid, unable to move, like she herself had drowned in the freezing waters of the Atlantic. Her gaze settled upon the last letter Marie sent which stood propped against the hurricane lamp on her nightstand. Next she let her eyes travel to the photograph of her father and mother. It was her father's eyes that seemed transfixed on her own. Even in a photograph the Vicar of Swardeston seemed to be preaching service and responsibility. His expression bore no smile, only stern eyes frozen in the photographic image; but the eyes said so much. She looked towards the window, outside of which lay occupied Belgium. It was with a tired, grieving hand across her forehead that she attempted to bring herself back to what needed to be done—in spite of personal loss or perhaps because of it.

A full moon lit the rain splattered glass of her window. Like tiny eyes watching her the droplets of water stared into the room and then slid away. Across the Avenue a metal drain pipe glistened in the evening's illumination and the taping of rain on the rooftops reminded her of far away soldiers' footsteps marching into obscurity. Somewhere a church bell chimed matins.

Edith continued sitting trance-like wondering how she would proceed with her dangerous work. Her door swung open with such force that the knob banged against the side wall. Four German Secret Police officers entered like a wave. Ignoring her presence each one went to a different corner of the room and began to search: walls, carpets, drawers. von Bissing himself strolled in slowly and moved leisurely to where Edith sat.

"Yes, we are searching again. Somehow I know we will never find anything here. You are a smart woman, Madame Cavell."

Edith didn't answer. She turned her head slowly away and watched the officers go through her closets.

"I have good news for you, Miss Cavell. In a way you will be getting your Institute back."

"Getting it back?"

"Yes. The High Command has deemed that they will allow the Red Cross sole management of the hospital."

Edith took a moment to assess the news. "Could that be to sway world opinion away from the facts. I have heard about the Geneva Convention's protests in respect to the German gas attacks at Ypres."

"The only assessment I am interested in is the one that comes from the High Command in Berlin. We care nothing for the Geneva Convention's opinion nor for the world's for that matter. The Red Cross made a request and Berlin accepted."

"When does the transition occur?"

"Tomorrow. Some of our German nurses will be replaced by Belgians and Swiss."

von Bissing glanced at each of the four officers who one by one shook their heads signifying that they found nothing.

"As I expected."

Edith straightened her posture in controlled victory.

"I will be watching you more closely now, Miss Cavell. You will not be able to hide behind the Red Cross forever."

"I have nothing to hide, General."

von Bissing nodded to his men to leave and then he strolled out as slowly as he entered.

✳

Helen Rosset stood in the doorway.

Edith knew about the Rosset woman. She studied the records of the young nurse and was aware of her qualifications. She made her judgement—and a not favorable judgement—of Helen Rosset by sight. She saw before her a beautiful, vain, flirtatious woman who seemed to be happy despite the circumstances of German occupation. Edith wondered where the compassion lay that prompted Helen Rosset to become a nurse and come to Berkendael to learn more. She recalled Sister White's warning that the woman could not be trusted.

"You are up rather late, Sister."

"I heard them leave, Matron Cavell."

"Don't concern yourself," Edith said, picking up some of the clothes the searching officers left strewn about the floor.

"I know what you think of me, Matron Cavell."

Edith raised her eyes and looked at Helen. "I am only concerned with your work, Sister."

"I look at the German men as men and I make no apologies for being interested in men. You may think what you like, even think me a whore, but I know myself. I can tell you that I am in this life for whatever pleasure I can take from it, but I would never betray my country."

Edith placed her ransacked clothes back in the closet while formulating a response. She realized that the war affected her more than she thought. She looked at everyone as a possible informer. The strain obviously took root in her soul. Sister Helen began to speak again.

"I know what you are doing, Matron Cavell."

"Do you?"

"Yes, I do. You do not need to play the part of the British Headmistress with me. I want to help you."

"Close the door, Sister."

Edith waited until the door closed shut.

"What do you know?"

"You forget that I am not as domesticated as the other sisters. I come and go at all hours. I see things and I am not stupid."

"What do you intend to do about it?"

"Nothing. I told you I want to help."

Edith looked at Helen and realized where the compassion that she once thought lacking in this young Belgian lay: in her eyes. Helen displayed the same sadness around the eyes that Edith became accustomed to looking at each time she gazed in the mirror. She knew that she must trust again. This would be the moment when she could kill the root of suspicion thriving and growing in her heart. Did the Vicar teach her to be this way? He would be ashamed.

"It is dangerous work and I do not wish to jeopardize your safety. I appreciate your offer, but I must leave things as they are."

"I am acquainted with many German soldiers, Matron Cavell, as you are aware. They talk when they are drunk and they are often drunk. They know what is going on here, or at least they suspect something. The Institute is to be put under surveillance. It may already be so."

Edith took a deep breath.

Helen softened her voice. "Why don't you make arrangements to escape yourself. Let me take your place."

"I cannot do that."

"Then please let me help you. This is my country. I use these Germans as they use me, but I prefer the Belgian men. I too want Belgium to be as it once was."

Edith took a moment to answer. "I will think of something you can do," she said, her eyes drifting to the letter from Madame Depage. "Please, get some rest. I have much to think about. We will talk again in the morning."

"Thank you, Matron Cavell. Goodnight."

Edith watched the door close. She felt everything closing in on her. The Germans are conducting surveillance. And didn't Herman Capiau once warn that she might be betrayed by someone she knew?

Chapter Twenty-Four

"What are the Germans planning to do?" Edith asked herself, while the oil lamp burned dimly on her desk and she wrote to Evaline. One friend in forty-nine years, Edith told herself. Why am I so solitary a woman? She realized that it might be that trait which would keep her alive and that trait which allowed her to save the lives of over two hundred allied soldiers so far. And still more were coming. With every soldier that passed through the doors of Berkendael and made it to Holland she knew she did God's work.

The representatives of the Red Cross arrived and all German nurses were transferred to other hospitals in Brussels. A staff of Belgian, Swiss, and Dutch sisters arrived and Edith was given full charge of the Institute. Where the sympathies of these new sisters lay was in little doubt, but Edith remained cautious. She couldn't help but wonder if von Bissing wasn't setting her up so he could bring the Red Cross in as accomplices.

On the afternoon of May 9th Capiau came and, using the newly arrived Red Cross as a cover, brought fourteen British soldiers dressed as Red Cross volunteers. This group of soldiers were all from British Territorial divisions and all were hardened, career military men. They seemed deadened to the fear around them and consequently a danger to their own safety. Two of the corporals got drunk the first night and the fighting almost spilled onto the Avenue outside.

"Do I have to remind you all that we are in occupied Belgium and not some tavern in Nottingham?" Edith admonished. She went to the highest ranking officer there, a sergeant major.

"They're just letting off steam, Miss. Life in the trenches wears a man down. I'll keep them in line from here on in," the sergeant-major said, breaking up the two men who began the fight and ordering them to their beds.

Sister Helen, standing at the door where she just entered the Institute, moved over to where Edith stood. "Can I speak with you, Matron Cavell? In your office?"

Edith waited until the last soldier left the room. "Certainly, Sister. I'm on my way there to prepare tomorrow's lecture."

Edith barely closed the door when Helen spoke: "von Bissing has the Institute under surveillance."

"Are you quite sure?"

"Yes. I have been seeing von Bissing's aide."

Edith went to her desk and took some paper from a drawer. She scratched a brief message and handed it to Sister Helen.

"You did say that you wanted to help, Sister?'

"Yes, I do."

"Take this to the address on the envelope. It is the home of Phillipe Baucq. He must get word to the others that we are being watched. Too many soldiers are under our roof at the moment and I have much to do to attend to them. They will need food and guides. Tell Baucq to send word to Capiau that we must move all the soldiers out of Berkendael as quickly as possible. I cannot tell you any more, Sister, and please do not ask any questions. Just deliver my message and come back here as fast as you can."

"Yes, Matron Cavell, and thank you for trusting me."

Chapter Twenty-Five

Sergeant Uber walked the streets of Brussels. His first night off in two years. He had nowhere to go, but to be free of the barracks and out from under the constant talk of the war came as a relief.

"I wonder how much longer I will be able to take it." He spoke his thoughts out loud as he walked. His companion, Sergeant Glosser, recovering from being too near an exploding shell still hadn't regained his hearing. Uber liked to walk with the man because he could unburden himself without having to worry about what he said being repeated to the other men.

Brussels was quiet and the night air hung heavy with misty rain. They both wore long great coats that covered their uniforms and gave them the appearance of Belgian merchants on their way home.

"Sometimes I am so embarrassed and ashamed of my affinity with the French. With a mother born in Paris and a German father who died when I was four I sometimes feel closer to the French than the Germans."

Sergeant Glosser smiled, but Uber knew the man heard nothing.

Uber continued, "I never entertained, mind you, that there was any other choice of which side I would fight for. The German Empire is where my home is; where my wife is, and our baby." Uber let the misty rain cover his face and didn't bother to wipe it off. It hid the tears from his companion. After all Sergeant Glosser's eyes were fine. Uber still hadn't seen the newborn girl that they named Yvette in honor of his mother, but whom they decided to refer to as Eva, so none of her future German childhood friends could mock her French name.

Sergeant Glosser noticed the red lamppost and the woman in the short skirt standing underneath it. With a wink he left Uber on his own.

Uber continued on alone and remembered the story told by his mother that they had relatives in Brussels, a second cousin named Carl Fergét who owned a tavern on the Rue de la Culture not far from Berkendael of all places. He recalled photographs exchanged and holiday letters sent. Would the man know him? He was family after all. Would there be ill feelings?

Uber moved through the thickening mist towards the address he remembered. He climbed the steps leading to a front door where a sign had been removed, the imprint of which left a square of new maroon bricks where the sign once was hung. He knocked. A peephole opened.

"Is there a Carl Fergét here?"

"Who is asking?" a gruff voice responded.

"His cousin Hans Uber. Son of Yvette Moule."

The door opened quickly and a strong arm pulled him in.

"Yvette's boy," the man said.

Uber left his coat on, to cover the uniform and his uncertainty of how it would be taken.

"I am Carl Fergét," the man said. His eyes showed that he caught a glimpse of the German uniform. "That's all right, boy. I know where your allegiance lies. It is not to divide a family. You are not responsible."

"I am sorry," Uber said, as if he personally held the blame for Belgium being occupied.

Carl nodded and cleaned a table. "Sit. I will bring you a hot meal," Carl attempted to speak in German, but abandoned the idea and the conversation progressed in French.

"Is your mother well, Carl?"

"Yes."

"And you, Hans? Married? Children?"

"My wife gave birth to a girl during the Battle of Tanneberg," Uber said, realizing that his life was now marked not by days or months, but by battles and military matters. "I still haven't seen her," he added.

"You will," Carl said, in a comforting voice as if no ideology divided them. They were blood.

"Are you sure you must go, Hans?"

"It has been two hours. I must report back. I am sorry. I hope it will all be over soon. Is there anything I can do for you?"

"I get by. Take care of yourself and send me a photograph of your baby."

The two men hugged, each of them knowing that in a matter of moments they would resume their roles as belonging on different sides of an insane war. Carl hugged his cousin once more and then went into the backroom.

Uber walked towards the door. He was about to leave when he decided to sit for a moment at a darkened table to try and sort his emotions before joining the ranks of the victors over an occupied enemy. How did this all happen? He was aware of the assassination of Archduke Ferdinand. He knew of the clash of imperialistic programs. He understood the entangled alliances that choked Europe. What he didn't comprehend was the bloodshed; the death. Did anyone want this? Will anyone be able to stop it?

A woman entered quietly and closed the door while holding the handle to prevent any noise as the latch clicked into place. She called out, "Mr. Fergét?"

Carl came out rubbing his hands on a towel.

"I was just closing," he said, and then recognized the woman. "Sister Helen."

"Edith asked me to come. We have some new men arriving. We will need woolen clothing, boots, overcoats, anything warm for when they go to the frontier before entering Holland."

"She thinks I have a store and forgets that I am only a connection to the black market. Tell her not to worry; she will have what she needs."

Sister Helen, at the door, whispered back, "Cabbages, leeks, cheese."

"I'll see what I can do," Carl said. The door closed and he returned to the backroom.

Uber waited a moment, pulled up his collar, and entered the Belgian night quietly.

Chapter Twenty-Six

*A*blazing light illuminated the sky where a shell exploded nearby. The brightness entered through the French windows like an unwanted guest. de Croy stood in the room that for years served as his parents' drawing room, where the aristocracy met in frivolous social displays as if their lifestyle were sacred and would never end. So much changed and de Croy stood alone in the room that became his headquarters. Where dinner parties were once planned by cooks and servants he now planned the escape of allied soldiers; soldiers fighting for a world which (even if they won and defeated the Germans) would never be the same again.

For a brief instant the explosion lit the house like a photographer's bulb illuminating the empty chairs, the deserted hallways, the rusty kitchen faucets, dusty floors, and tarnished serving trays. A few candles flickered. de Croy went about his business of collecting anything that might be incriminating. The Germans were getting too close. All his information relayed the same thing: they were aware of his activities. One final trip to Brussels needed to be made to warn Baucq and Cavell and then he would make his own escape into Holland—his work here completed. If he stayed he would be jeopardizing the lives of those he worked so hard to protect. He took a look around the rooms of the chateau. The white marble fireplace that once warmed his family and their guests remained unused so that the smoke from the chimney would not serve as a beacon to German soldiers out on patrol, but now he threw papers into the fire that consumed the incriminating documents he tossed into the flames. The doors that led into the ballroom stood open like a gaping mouth waiting for someone to enter. Over one of the sofas hung a portrait of Belgian peasants, pink faced and innocent to all that now took over their country.

de Croy blew out the candles and stood in the darkened doorway, wondering if he would ever return to this place of his youth and if he did return would anything be left standing.

Everything that once signified June and the coming of the Belgian summer seemed to be somehow absent. de Croy looked into the darkened countryside while the first signs of daylight appeared in the eastern sky. What exactly was different he couldn't tell except that there were less birds, fewer trees, an absence of hope in the air. de Croy sat huddled in back of the cart under a heavy blanket. He had his oil lantern lit low and wrote quickly. If the Germans found the information he was writing down many would lose their lives, but he had to take the chance. He needed to detail the workings of his organization so someone else, someone less known to the German Secret Police, could continue the work of aiding allied soldiers. This war showed no signs of slowing down and sometimes felt as if it would go on forever. de Croy planned to be there while his group in Brussels read his notes and then he would personally pick a successor and destroy everything he was now writing down. He extinguished the flame of his lantern and closed his eyes. The wheels rumbled underneath him, the Belgian countryside rolling into the past. Where his future lay was uncertain. He could be spending the rest of the war, perhaps the rest of his life, in Holland; unless the Germans found him first: then it would all end with a bullet.

Chapter Twenty-Seven

The avenue stirred with German soldiers. de Croy observed the commotion from a corner in the shadows. He hadn't much time. He must warn Baucq and Cavell, try and see that the escape organization continued without him, and then make an attempt at escape to Holland.

Something inside him held a presentiment of doom. He looked at his watch. A group of soldiers halted their march and a car pulled to the side. de Croy's worst fears were realized: the Germans were drawing closer to the home of Phillipe Baucq.

It was all over in a few moments. A battering ram caved Baucq's door in; soldiers entered; Baucq was taken out half-dressed and thrown into a car; a few high ranking officers carried out what appeared to be boxes of papers.

A few faces appeared in the upper windows of some houses along the avenue, but the street was now eerily deserted. A wind blew a few scraps of debris across the road and the door of Baucq's home swung precariously on one hinge.

Otto Mayer sat at his desk, his elbows on the file folders, his hands pressed together in a praying posture. One look into his cold, static eyes, however, left little doubt that he was not a praying man. The German Secret Police found no need for prayers. It was the Belgians who needed to pray. The weaker of the species needed to call on their God. Mayer peered over his fingertips while the door opened and someone pushed Phillipe Baucq in. The door slammed shut and Mayer motioned with his open palm for Baucq to take a seat.

Otto Mayer sat with a pretense of patience while a nervous, frightened Baucq, bleary eyed and bruised, looked around the room. Confusion and fear were predominate on Phillipe Baucq's face. Again Mayer held out an outstretched palm towards a chair close to the desk. Mayer was a small man with short arms and fingers. He wore a neatly pressed suit. Perfectly combed hair covered the top of his well rested face. The contrast with the prisoner Baucq seemed more pronounced since they kept Phillipe awake all night under interrogation. He rubbed his bruised left eye and sat down shakily. Mayer stood simultaneously as if on cue. The muscles in the German's jaw twitched giving him the appearance of one about to strike as soon as the time seemed right. He spread open the curtains and let in a bright stream of light. The reflection of sunlight onto Mayer's gold rimmed glasses made him appear to have no eyes, only light emanating from the deeply set eye sockets behind the lenses. Otto Mayer glared at Baucq seated there weary and about to pass out. His gaze fell onto the bruises on Baucq's face and he appeared to relish the sight of the blood. Mayer's lips parted in a smile that resembled more of a grimace, like one in pain.

"You are a stubborn man, Monsieur Baucq," Mayer spoke in French.

Phillipe could only manage to lift his head. He stared blankly past Mayer and out of the window into the Belgian daylight that he feared he would never enter again.

"What is even worse is that you are a stupid man. A man far too stupid to be stubborn. What you tell me now is only a formality, but it will determine if you live or die."

Baucq knew immediately what Mayer referred to. How careless I am to leave all those papers. Baucq remembered being dragged from his home by the Secret Police and how they gathered the evidence into a large box laughing and speaking in German as they did so. How many have I implicated by my negligence? Baucq wondered. How many death sentences have I signed?

de Croy spent the night in the barn of one of the safe houses he used in his escape organization. He rose before dawn with the memory of Phillipe Baucq's arrest still in his thoughts. It was a fitful night of dreams where he saw himself and Capiau and Cavell and all of the others being brought out of Baucq's home where they were shot on the street. Litter from the box of evidence, which the German's carried out during the arrest, were scattered about their bodies. He awoke in a cold sweat. He forced on his shoes hurrying to be on his way to Berkendael to warn Edith. de Croy peered out of the slats of the barn's wooden loft door and into the still murky darkness. He pulled his cap low over his eyes and moved quickly through the shadows.

The sky was overcast and the low clouds provided cover by prolonging the night's darkness and forestalling the light of dawn. Brussels lay quiet, but it wasn't the restful quiet of pre-dawn. An apprehensive silence filled the city. A silence that came from fear. de Croy felt that somehow he no longer walked in Belgium; that his footsteps echoed on German streets now. The German flag that hung over a government building; a grouping of German military lorries on a side street; a discarded German newspaper that blew across the pavement: all of it gave the signs of an occupied country. He did not want to leave Belgium this way. He wanted to fight on for freedom, but too many lives would be at risk if he stayed. He knew he must be cautious with the lives of others. The memory of the box of papers that the Germans carried out of Phillipe Baucq's home came to mind. He raised his eyes and saw a small, weak light (probably coming from a flickering candle) which gave the window of Edith's office a soft glow. A fading glow. Like the prospects of their future. She obviously got his message and she sat waiting for him.

Chapter Twenty-Eight

"Miss Cavell—Edith—you must listen. Berkendael has become too dangerous. Belgium has become too dangerous. You must leave with me immediately," de Croy pleaded.

Edith looked at him without speaking and her eyes moved unconsciously to her father's photograph on the wall. *Service to our fellow man…*

"You've done quite enough already. Over two hundred Allied soldiers have passed through these walls and on to Holland. Why jeopardize your life? Others will take over and carry on the work."

"I expect to be arrested," Edith stated, calmly. "Escape for me is futile. If I go they will search very persistently for me and then you too, and Herman, and the others, will be caught."

"I, too, will be searched for," de Croy reminded her.

"Yes, but the Germans do not know of your escape plans. It could be days before they know you are gone. They will search Mons and Wasmes first before they realize that you have been on to them and have left. As for me, how long do you think it will take von Bissing to comprehend that I have escaped? Remember I am under surveillance. They will begin their search within minutes. Don't you see that there is no hope for me?"

de Croy mulled it over. "We will still have time to get a head start if we leave now."

"When I don't give my lecture in the morning, or am not available to perform the administrative duties here, someone will inform. The

Germans will come quickly."

"I fear for your safety. Baucq has already been arrested," de Croy presented this last bit of news that he had been saving as a last resort to convince her to leave with him.

Edith's face tightened and she touched her buttoned collar. "Baucq? They have him?"

"Yes. I was there when they took him. I also saw the Germans carrying boxes of papers out of the house. I am afraid that Baucq has been careless."

"What papers did the Germans find at Phillipe's home? Could he have been so careless as to not have destroyed incriminating evidence?" Edith wondered out loud.

"They are disturbing questions. We cannot wait for the answers," de Croy said. He added, "I recall the night in the fields where Capiau voiced his misgivings about Baucq's absentminded ways. I am to blame if the Germans find anything. I should have listened to Herman. How many of my organization is in jeopardy at this moment?"

"Herman can take care of those in Mons and Wasmes. It is only Phillipe and I who are at risk here in Brussels," Edith commented, knowing that she and Baucq were now on their own.

"Somehow I feel that if Baucq were careless that carelessness will come to doom you, Edith. I must take you out of Belgium tonight," de Croy said with determination.

Edith thought of the times when she wanted to warn de Croy about the absentminded Baucq. It was too late now.

"Then it is certain. They will be coming for me."

"Won't you reconsider, Edith?" de Croy implored.

"No. I must stay. If only to keep them from you and the others. The Germans will arrest me, but what can they do? I am a nurse who is treating patients. If they prove that I have treated Allied soldiers I can also show that I have treated German ones as well. I am in charge of a Red Cross hospital. I am neutral as far as they can prove. I don't see what they can do other than deport me or make life unpleasant for me here."

A siren blew from the direction of the avenue. Edith and de Croy moved to either side of the window and peered out of the folds of the curtains. A black Mercedes sped up to the front entrance of Berkendael.

"You must leave. Take the side stairs. They lead to the alley. Go over the fence by the gardener's shed. I keep a bicycle there. Take it."

de Croy gave one last, silent and imploring look, but he knew it was futile to try and dissuade her. Without a word he rushed out of the door.

Edith turned to the window. A small man, neatly dressed, with wire rim glasses which reflected light, got out of the car. He signaled to an officer to intercept a Red Cross nurse who was carrying the day's incoming mail. The officer brought the small man the mailbag. He secured his glasses on the bridge of his nose and rummaged through the letters pulling out what appeared to be a postcard. He studied it, smiled, and tucked it into his breast pocket. With a sure gait he entered Berkendael.

Edith was surprised at the window when the door opened in a jolt. They must have quickened their pace to arrive at her door so quickly, she thought. Two German Secret Police officers stood on either side of her door while the small man walked in.

"You are under arrest, Madame," he announced in excellent French.

There was something peaceful about sitting in the cell beneath German General Headquarters. Edith felt almost relieved. She had been expecting the arrest to come and now it was as if everything fell into place. The man called Otto Mayer had been almost polite about it all. Very little words were spoken after being taken from Berkendael. Edith overheard from a guard communicating on the wireless that the Germans searched the Institute and found nothing. She felt satisfied knowing that she took the time to sew her diary into one of the cushions in Marie Depage's sitting room. It would never be found. If only Baucq acted as carefully.

Edith stood on her toes and peeked out of the iron grated window at the Belgian sky. She could see only patches of blue from the basement cell. She imagined she would be kept here for a matter of a few days, formally interrogated by von Bissing, and then deported to England; or perhaps kept under house arrest and allowed to continue her duties at Berkendael. After all this was war and nurses were needed.

Edith took a shawl and wrapped it around her shoulders. It hung loosely on her frame. She lost so much weight while she gave her food to the Allied soldiers and went without. The vicar's lessons were well learned. The damp, cold basement air crept into her bones reminding her of the English winters she left behind so many years ago and to which she might be returning to soon. The British fog and rain would be welcome compared to this compressed life in occupied Belgium. Yet, she would miss her work. She wondered where Doctor Depage was at this moment. The only consolation came from the fact that so much had been accomplished: over two hundred Allied soldiers taken into Holland; de Croy and Capiau presumably safe. The escape organization might even continue. Poor Phillipe, she suspected, would not fare as well. The Germans would send him to a work camp to serve out the remainder of the war. She looked around her cell at the bare mortar walls and for one strange moment she could see the photograph of her father that hung in her rooms at Berkendael. The vicar would have no qualms with her actions. She did as she was taught: served those less fortunate than herself. This cell was a reward, in a way, and set her free from having to live up to what her father constantly drilled into her. She felt free from responsibility for the first time in her life. When she would get back to England she would take a quiet post, perhaps as a night nurse or as an administrator of a small school for nurses. Who knew, perhaps one day she could return to Belgium. But would she want to? So many would be gone, so much would have changed. And what if Germany won the war? Better to tend a small English garden and live out the rest of her life in prayer and reflection.

Chapter Twenty-Nine

Otto Mayer looked up from his desk, his face tight, his eyes opened wide.

"What do you mean they are gone?"

"The chateau is empty. de Croy, Capiau, and the other leaders have escaped. We have men searching the area of Mons and Wasmes, but I believe they may have already reached Holland."

"You believe? Your job is not to believe, it is to make arrests," Mayer spoke through clenched teeth, his jaw muscles twitching.

"We did manage to arrest thirty-five members of their organization."

"And do you think that is satisfactory?"

"No, sir."

"Pack your kit, Kruger."

"Am I going to try and intercept them on the border?"

"No," Mayer smiled the grimace of a smile peculiar to him, "you are being sent to the Western Front. I am writing the orders of transfer now. I should have never left you to do what I myself should have taken care of."

"But, sir—"

"Dismissed," Mayer said, calmly without looking up.

Kruger took a stunned moment before moving towards the door.

"Wait one moment, Kruger," Mayer said, softly.

"Yes, sir," Kruger answered, hopefully. Perhaps Herr Mayer had a change of heart.

"Does the Cavell woman know that her organization's leaders have escaped to Holland?"

"No, sir."

"Good. Dismissed. I want you on the midnight train," Mayer said, coldly.

Mayer paced his office with a stack of papers in his hand. His aide stood nervously at the door waiting to be dismissed.

"These reports say nothing about the workings of the escape organization. Thirty Five men arrested and I have nothing."

"We have interrogated them thoroughly. They know nothing. All of them are part of the organization, but neither knew of the others. They had specific roles along the escape route, independently. This de Croy is very smart in the way he set his group up."

Mayer glared back at him. "Then we must be smarter. Dismissed."

Mayer entered Edith's cell, alone. For a long moment he watched her recumbent on the small cot in the corner, under the grated window. With his toe he gave the frame of the cot a push. Edith woke quickly, startled. Mayer stood staring at her to unnerve and intimidate her. He had nothing but her fear and uncertainty to work with.

"I want to share some news with you, Madame. We have captured thirty five members of your organization. They are making full confessions now. We also have all the leaders."

Edith stood and faced Mayer.

"Tell me, Madame. How many Allied soldiers did you help to escape?"

"I did not ask the nationality of those I attended to in hospital."

"You worked against the German Empire."

"I worked for humanity, of all kinds. I treated men, not soldiers. They ceased to be soldiers as soon as they were wounded and removed from the front."

"Did you feed the Allied soldiers?"

"If patients were hungry I fed them. Just as I dispensed the medicine they needed."

"Belgium is under German occupation and all resources are to be handed over for our use. If you fed them you must have used valuable food needed at the front," Mayer spoke calmly, and kept touching his breast pocket.

"I remind you that I am in charge of a Red Cross hospital. We are neutral."

"We both of us know that is not true. You must cooperate, Madame."

"I have nothing more to say."

"You give me no alternative but to place you in solitary confinement."

Chapter Thirty

Sergeant Uber stood at attention while Otto Mayer leafed through his notes. Mayer took off his glasses, wiped them clean, put them back on, straightened his tie. Uber felt as if he were not in the room. If Mayer intended to remind him of his subservience he succeeded.

Mayer finally spoke.

"Sergeant Uber. I have held Miss Cavell in solitary confinement for nine weeks now and still I have nothing. You were a patient at Berkendael were you not?"

"Yes, sir," Uber answered, knowing full well that Mayer held his records in front of him.

"What did you learn there?"

"Learn?"

"Are you aware of the fact that Allied soldiers have been brought to Berkendael before their final escape into Holland?"

"I have heard the stories."

"Stories?" Mayer began to raise his voice, but checked himself."

He smiled. The smile that everyone who saw it took to be an expression of discomfort not humor. "I have read in psychology books stories of soldiers who when wounded and cared for by a nurse fall in love with her. Anyone who aids a wounded man takes on a certain familiarity, but I need not remind you that we are at war."

"No, sir. I need no reminders of that."

"Then you must have seen something that caused suspicion while you were at Berkendael?"

Uber thought of the late nights when the ward slept and he lay awake. He remembered the smell of food being cooked after midnight, well after the patients had been fed. He recalled the beds full with men who for some reason never spoke. Men that he was told were German soldiers. And then suddenly they were gone. The night he overheard the sister from Berkendael requesting certain supplies from his cousin Carl Fergét particularly haunted him.

"No, sir. I observed nothing to be suspicious of."

When Mayer entered the solitary confinement cell he switched on the light that hung over her bed and unlocked the shutters to let in sunlight. Edith raised her arm to shelter the light that stung her eyes. She squinted when Mayer addressed her.

"You could have been out of here and free. Instead you have wasted nine weeks. For nothing."

"Am I to be freed now?"

"I am afraid not. All thirty five of your colleagues have confessed," Mayer lied. He continued the bluff, "I also have testimony, damaging testimony for you, from a man who was a patient at Berkendael. Do you remember Sergeant Uber?"

Edith remembered the man who spoke French because his mother was French. Their secret he told her. She felt saddened more by the news of Uber than of the confessions of thirty five of de Croy's men.

"I am afraid they will all be executed. Unless…"

Edith stared into the sunlight and then into Mayer's eyes. "I will tell you everything."

Chapter Thirty-One

*T*he subdued military courtroom, convened in one of the old courthouses of Brussels, echoed even the slightest of sounds. The room, built with the intention of accommodating many, seemed empty with only the few who were present huddled in the front near the judge's bench. The thirty five members of de Croy's escape organization, none of whom confessed, were tried quickly. Some of them were already removed and executed. It had been decided that Edith Cavell would merit more attention, if only as an example to the occupied nation. von Bissing and Mayer sat at a long table with the prosecuting attorney.

Edith sat alone with her lawyer, an aging attorney long retired, summoned hastily by the American ambassador. Spain joined the United States in demanding clemency.

"This British woman, Edith Cavell, is charged with crimes against the Empire, your honor," the prosecutor said in a clear voice, but it seemed to waver when he looked at von Bissing and added, "We demand the death penalty."

"Continue," the judge said.

"She has assisted allied soldiers to escape from Belgium into Holland so they can resume arms against Germany."

Edith's lawyer stood and supported himself on the table top with aging hands and weary arms.

"Miss Cavell is a nurse—"

"She has confessed," the prosecutor interrupted.

Undaunted, Edith's defender continued, "It is her duty, her occupation to help those in need."

"To treat the wounded. Not to help them escape."

"Is there proof of that? I know for a fact that she has also treated German soldiers."

The judge glanced at a restless von Bissing. The General nodded to him and he spoke, "It is the duty of the court to sentence her to death."

Edith's lawyer seemed to summon a reserve of youthful energy. With a reddened face his voice rose, "Miss Cavell may be guilty of committing an offence against German military law, but that is not a capital offence."

Mayer summoned the prosecuting attorney to the table. He reached into his breast pocket and handed the lawyer a postcard sized paper. Edith recalled the day she saw him take the card from the mailbag in front of Berkendael.

"I have here a postcard from a soldier, Private Harold Jenkins. It is posted from London. In it he thanks Miss Cavell for helping him into Holland. He hopes to be well enough to come to Belgium and thank her personally one day. Presumably he will be carrying a gun when he comes here, Miss Cavell," the prosecutor turned to speak directly to Edith. He then turned to face the judge, "To help soldiers so they can fight us another day is a capital offence," the man said, but there was no gloating in his voice and he didn't look at Edith or her attorney.

The judge wiped his brow and took another look at von Bissing. "My sentence: death by firing squad at dawn on October 12, 1915."

Chapter Thirty-Two

*T*he knock on his door came with a light touch of uncertainty. Mayer smiled and appeared not to notice when Sergeant Uber entered. Sitting at his desk Mayer held a cup and saucer before him and leaned back in his chair sipping the strong German coffee laced with schnapps. For him it seemed a reward and he wore his grimace of a smile, which seemed to harbor pain, with a certain satisfaction.

"You wanted to see me, Herr Mayer?"

"Yes. You have heard the verdict?"

"I have."

"I am still wondering why you were never able to corroborate any information for me; you being a patient at Berkendael."

"I witnessed nothing to report, sir."

"No matter, Sergeant Uber. I know that you are a loyal German. You will be allowed a great honor."

"An honor?"

"Yes. Corporal Brager has taken ill. You will replace him tomorrow."

"I ate breakfast with Brager this morning. He is fine."

Mayer put down his cup and saucer and leaned forward over his desk. "He is ill. You will have the honor of taking his place on the firing squad."

"I am not a marksman, Herr Mayer," Uber protested.

"You will be there all the same. Perhaps it will be your bullet that finds a place in Miss Cavell."

"Sir, my other duties."

"It is arranged. You will report one hour before dawn on October 12th. The day after tomorrow. Dismissed."

"Miss Cavell."

"I am over here, chaplain," Edith answered, emerging from the shadows of her cell and turning up the wick of the oil lamp.

"I thought perhaps you might want to talk."

"Yes, father."

"I'm sorry, do you prefer a priest?"

Edith stared blankly a moment. "No, chaplain. I was thinking of someone else."

"The American and Spanish ambassadors are still protesting the ruling, but I fear they will not change the verdict," Chaplain Gahan whispered. "You are an admirable woman. God will reward you," he added.

Edith smiled. A small bit of light from a guard's torch came through the barred door window and fell on the floor before her then disappeared as the man continued his rounds.

"Do you have any messages for anyone?" Gahan asked.

"No, there is no one. Evaline will be receiving a letter I posted shortly before I was arrested; Doctor Depage, if he is alive, will know my thoughts would be with him. Mother is gone. I have no one."

Chaplain Gahan took out a pad and pen. "I will note that you sacrificed yourself for England. There will be citizens at home who will be wanting a last piece of news. You are greatly admired, Edith. You are an inspiration for all patriots of Britain."

"Standing as I do, in view of God and eternity, I realize that patriotism is not enough: I must have no hatred or bitterness towards anyone."

Gahan let the words settle and then with a sigh he rose and signaled for the guard that his meeting ended. He touched Edith on the shoulder and could not look back when the door closed.

✳

Dawn of October 12th broke with a feeble light in an overcast sky. A piercing wind blew from the west. At the National Rifle Range on the outskirts of Brussels two firing squads, eight men on each, stood waiting. They stomped their feet to stay warm in the autumn chill, moving in their places to keep the blood circulating and to hold anxiety in check. Sergeant Uber shifted the most, more in an attempt to disguise his shaking knees than as a means of staying warm. He felt his whole body tremble as the car pulled up slowly out of the mist. Two guards brought Edith out dressed in her nurses' uniform. He wondered if she recognized him. He thought she did, but there was not a trace of fear or anger on her face.

The captain gave the order for them to stand at attention and assume a firing posture.

In the slight rays of sunshine that escaped from the harsh sky Uber saw the traces of blood, dried and browning, where Baucq and others had fallen the day before. He heard the muffled orders. It all was happening as if in a dream. The next moment his eyes focused on Edith who was already standing at the wall.

More orders came. He was vaguely aware that he had still not raised his rifle. The command was shouted and shots were fired. He remained frozen. He watched her fall, like a leaf from a tree, softly. Her fragile body hadn't even allowed for a thud when she hit the ground. He still stood rigid when he heard his name called.

"Uber!"

He could not respond, but managed to turn his head to face the captain.

"You refused your duty. You are a coward and a traitor."

The rifles were now pointed at him.

He heard his mother's voice singing in French and felt a punch when the shots were fired. He sensed the slightest touch of earth on his cheek and the faint sound of a fall before it all went black.

Epilogue

*T*he ink on the armistice had been dry for over a year, yet the tensions and repercussions of the long war still hung in the air when Edith's body was returned to England. In a week, Christmas of 1919 would arrive and the world would try and find peace.

Private Harold Jenkins moved solemnly to Westminster Abbey while the great bells sounded. He asked himself the same question he had been asking for years: why did I send that postcard?

The first signs of spring fell in silence as Chaplain Gahan brought Doctor Depage to the spot. They spent the early morning at the National Rifle Range and Gahan allowed Depage all the time he needed to stand in silence and ponder the events of that day four years earlier. Next they went to the shallow grave near the Rifle Range—the hole still lay exposed and uncovered like a gaping mouth with its jaw dropped open in death. It was almost too much for Depage. He steadied himself on the Chaplain's arm.

"They exhumed the body last week and brought her back to England for reburial."

Depage wiped a tear knowing that there would be no burial for Marie. She was lost. "I want to go back to Berkendael and see where they buried Francois."

The carriage pulled up to Westminster Abbey through the throng standing solemn and quiet. A light rain fell. King George V exited the carriage and greeted Prime Minister Lloyd George.

Boger whispered to Meachin, "Shall we go inside."

"No, I've decided to stay here," Meachin answered. "Too many memories," he added. He let the rain hit his face. "On second thought let's. We owe her that."

Sister White sat in the very last pew. She listened to the sermons and speeches and wondered what the years of 1914-1918 were sacrificed for.

The sun rose in Bavaria as the coffin was lowered into the section of ground that faced east. The priest spoke softly to the young woman, "He is home now Mrs. Uber."

"Yes," the young woman said, holding the baby he never saw. In a quiet voice she asked of the priest, "Do you know any prayers in French?"